BBC
DOCTOR WHO

BBC CHILDREN'S BOOKS

UK I USA I Canada I Ireland I Australia
India I New Zealand I South Africa
BBC Children's Books are published by Puffin Books,
part of the Penguin Random House group of companies
whose addresses can be found at global.penguinrandomhouse.com.
www.penguin.co.uk   www.puffin.co.uk   www.ladybird.co.uk

Penguin
Random House
UK

First published 2016
001

All I Want for C: by Colin Brake,
The Christmas In   :hard Dungworth,
Sontar's Little H   by Gary Russell,
The Grotto written   k, *The Red Bicycle*
written by Gary R   y Scott Handcock,

First Do   :work by
Melissa   stound,
Fourth Doctor a   is – Pickled Ink,
Sixth D   work by
Charlie Sut   dvocate Art,
Ninth Doctor a   Captain Kris –
Good Illustr   nternational,

LONDON BOROUGH OF WANDSWORTH		
9030 00005 5383 2		
Askews & Holts	18-May-2017	
JF	£12.99	
	WW17001553	

Twelfth Doctor artwork by Tom Duxbury – Artist Partners

Printed in Great Britain by Clays Ltd, St Ives plc
A CIP catalogue record for this book is available from the British Library

ISBN: 978–1–405–92895–3

BBC

DOCTOR WHO

TWELVE DOCTORS OF CHRISTMAS

PUFFIN

CONTENTS

ALL I WANT
FOR CHRISTMAS

Written by Jacqueline Rayner

Illustrated by Nick Harris

They followed their footsteps back to the TARDIS.
Here and there, little paw prints belonging to some unknown animal crossed their path, but otherwise the snow was untouched. No humans, or even near-humans, lived in this land. Their visit had been a short one – a search for the minerals needed to power a machine that the Doctor was working on, that was all. A success, for once, with no danger to complicate matters.

'Pine needles and crisp, clean air. It smells of Christmas!' Ian said wistfully.

Barbara didn't look at Ian as he spoke. Her eyes were focused on something that wasn't there, some sort of distant memory. 'Do you remember the smell of Stir-up Sunday?

Warm spices and brandy.'

'Stir up, we beseech thee, O Lord,' said Ian, and the two schoolteachers smiled, but their smiles had sadness underneath.

The young girl walking between them turned from one to the other, frowning. 'I don't understand,' she said.

Of course it was Barbara who answered. She could never resist a chance to educate. 'A custom of our time, Vicki,' she said. 'When you heard those words in the prayer for the day at church, you knew it was time to make the Christmas pudding.'

'Oh,' said Vicki. 'I see.' Then she paused for a second and added, almost casually, 'What's a Christmas pudding?'

'Vicki!' both Barbara and Ian cried out in astonishment.

'Oh, I've heard of Christmas,' the girl said, oblivious to their horror. 'But I'm not quite sure what a pudding is.'

So Barbara told her, with Ian joining in. The making of the Christmas pudding: nutmeg and cinnamon and sugar, orange zest and candied peel, almonds and suet and breadcrumbs, all mixed together with a good dollop of brandy.

'You'd put in a sixpence too,' said Ian. 'Then everyone would stir the mixture and make a wish.'

Barbara smiled. 'My mum had a sixpence, a proper

silver one, with Queen Victoria's head on it. That went into
the pudding every year, but the finder didn't get to keep it.
Dad would give out a new one instead, the ones with only a
bit of silver in them.'

'Of course, since the war, sixpences don't have any silver
in them at all,' said Ian. 'They're made of cupro-nickel now.'
And, because he could never pass up an opportunity to share
his knowledge with a pupil either, whether in school or not, he
added, 'That's an alloy of copper and nickel.' He didn't seem
to notice he was still talking about 'now' – meaning the early
1960s – when in fact they were on a planet that could have
been millions of years in the past or the future from then.

The memories were flowing, and neither Ian nor
Barbara could turn them off. Visions of Christmases long
gone danced in their heads.

'Mum and Dad would decorate the tree overnight with
paper chains and candles.' That was Ian again. 'You just had
to hope that the candles wouldn't set fire to the paper chains.'

'Did you ever have a snapdragon?' Barbara cut in. 'We
used to love snatching almonds and raisins from the flames.
Your fingers got burned, but it was worth it!

'There was one time, during the war, I didn't think
there'd be anything in my stocking. Mum had explained how
even Santa didn't have enough coupons to get sweets for

everyone on his list. And then, on Christmas morning, there
it was! An apple, nuts, a peg doll and a huge bag of barley
sugar. Oh, I'd known for years that there was no Santa, just
Mum and Dad play-acting, but all the same I believed in
magic, then, for a while.'

'We'd watch the queen's speech – or listen to the king
on the radio, before that – then play games. Charades,
consequences, and blind man's buff!'

Vicki listened, enthralled. 'It all sounds *marvellous!*'
she said.

'Yes, it was,' said Barbara wistfully. 'I wonder if we will
ever see Christmas again. If I had one wish –'

'Don't say it!' Ian cried out. 'Remember what happens
when you stir the pudding! If you tell people your wish,
it won't come true!' And, although he was laughing, and
although a man of science obviously couldn't believe in
wishes, it sounded for a second as though he really meant it.

The Doctor was already at the controls when they
entered the TARDIS.

Barbara shook the snow off her boots and hung up her
woollen coat. 'Time for bed, Vicki,' she said.

'Oh, but I want to hear more about Christmas!'
begged Vicki.

'What's all this about Christmas?' asked the Doctor.

'We were just indulging in a spot of nostalgia,' Ian
replied. 'Reminiscing about long ago.'

'The past is never long ago when you have a time
machine!' said the Doctor.

No one replied. But both Barbara and Ian were thinking
the same thing: a childhood Christmas is further away
than Ancient Rome, if your time machine can't actually be
controlled . . .

That night, Barbara dreamed of her mother, who she hoped
to see again one day, and of her father, who she would never
see again. How could she bear to, even if the Doctor could
take her to a time when he was still alive? She always carried
a photo of him, a studio portrait on a postcard, faded and
tattered now. For a time, after she'd been snatched from her
life, she'd looked at it every day, the only link to her family, a
connection across the stars. Recently she gazed at it
less and less, and now she felt obscurely guilty about that, as
if her acceptance of their strange travels somehow meant she
didn't care any more about those she'd left behind.

When she awoke, she realised she'd been crying in her
sleep. Vicki wasn't in the next bed, which was good. The
girl had lost so much: her mother, her father, her home,
everything she'd ever known . . . Barbara knew that crying

because her dad would never again put a sugar mouse into the toe of her stocking seemed an indulgence compared to Vicki's much greater losses.

Barbara made her way to the control room, expecting to find Vicki there, or at least the Doctor, but it was empty. She could tell they weren't in flight, and looked up at the scanner to see what was outside the ship. It just showed white snow gleaming in the darkness. No . . . a closer look revealed footprints. Footprints in the snow! They were still in the same place.

Vicki came running into the control room. 'You're up! At last! Come on!' She took hold of Barbara's arm, dragging her towards the main doors.

'Why so excited?' asked Barbara. 'There's nothing interesting out there. We saw that yesterday.'

Vicki dropped hold of her arm and looked at Barbara disappointedly, as though she was the teacher and Barbara the student. 'We're not *there* any more. Come and see. Now!'

Ian and the Doctor joined them – Ian from his own sleeping quarters further inside the TARDIS, and the Doctor through the doors from outside, which he closed behind him. 'Nothing to see out there,' he said. 'We might as well take off.'

'No!' yelled Vicki, putting herself between the Doctor and the controls. 'We have to go outside! We have to!'

'But it's just snow and trees,' protested Ian. 'I'm with the Doctor. There's no point in staying here.'

'It's not the same place!' Vicki insisted. 'It's somewhere new.'

'No no, my child,' said the Doctor. 'It's just the same snow. Just the same trees.'

But Barbara had been watching the scanner. 'I see something! I see lights!' She turned to the Doctor suspiciously. 'Why don't you want us to see what's *really* out there?'

'Because we haven't moved,' the Doctor repeated tetchily. 'There is nothing out there.'

But his bluster was unconvincing. Suddenly Barbara darted at the door control. 'I need to see for myself!' she said.

The doors swung open. Cold wind whipped through the control room, and brought other things with it.

A scent of spices and candlewax.

A peal of bells.

Voices, distant and sweet, singing of a baby in a manger.

Barbara ran through the doors. She didn't stop for her coat or scarf. She just kept running towards the sound. There were lights now, the harlequin lights of flickering candle flames through stained glass. And suddenly she found herself outside a church: the source of the lights and the sounds and the scents. There was enough light through the windows to allow her to read the noticeboard outside the church doors:

St Swithun's. Midnight Mass.

11.30 p.m. Tuesday 24 December 1963.

1963.

The date struck Barbara like a blow.

This was her year – hers and Ian's!

They were *home*!

Ian joined her. He'd brought her coat and now draped it over her shoulders, but it made no difference to Barbara, who hadn't felt the cold. She pointed at the notice, unable to bring herself to speak.

'*Home . . .*' whispered Ian in amazement. Then he let out a loud cry of delight, dancing around in a circle. 'Home! We're home!'

'And only a month since we left,' said Barbara, forcing her mouth to form the words. Tears pricked at her eyes, but she was not someone who cried. Certainly not twice in one day, anyway.

The Doctor and Vicki came along too, now. Vicki was almost jumping with excitement, but the Doctor didn't look happy. Barbara turned on him. 'We're home,' she said. 'Ian and I, we're home. Is that why you didn't want us to come out here? You didn't want us to see? You didn't want us to leave?'

The Doctor looked furious, which meant he was feeling

defensive. 'Not at all,' he snapped. 'I merely didn't want you to get your hopes up.'

'What do you mean?' demanded Ian.

'Well, all of this! Christmas! Christmas 1963! And in England, no less. You think it's a coincidence we land here only hours after you've been talking of such things?'

'Maybe the TARDIS heard us somehow,' said Ian.

'Or maybe someone did,' added Barbara quietly. She knew that the wish she'd made last night – *Oh please, let me have Christmas again, Christmas at home* – had turned into a prayer halfway through.

'Oh, very well,' said the Doctor with a sniff. 'Investigate if you must. But don't lose sight of the idea that this may be a trap!'

'I'm sure it isn't,' said Vicki.

Barbara pushed open the door of the church and they went in. Warmth enveloped them. A few faces turned to see the latecomers, but no one seemed shocked or surprised. Barbara picked up four hymn books from the pile near the door and handed them out, but Ian was already joining in with 'O Little Town of Bethlehem'.

The hopes and fears of all the years. Barbara's hopes had been realised; her fears were over. She was home.

At the end of the service, the four travellers lingered at

the back of the church. As the vicar walked towards the door, Barbara moved to intercept him.

'I don't believe I've had the pleasure,' the old man said. 'Visiting for Christmas, are you?'

Barbara shook her head. 'No. Trying to get home for Christmas, but . . .'

She couldn't think how to finish that sentence, but the vicar finished it for her. 'Snowed in, I assume? Yes, it's such a shame. All the roads blocked, and the telephone lines down too.'

A deep breath. So near home, and yet so far. But what did it matter? Christmas was only a date. A further delay would only make their eventual homecoming all the sweeter.

'Is there a hotel?' Barbara asked. 'Or a boarding house? Somewhere nearby we could stay?'

The vicar was shaking his head sadly as a man and woman joined them. Older than Barbara. Probably older than Barbara's mother. 'Excuse me for interrupting,' the woman said. 'Do I understand you're stuck here, unable to get home?'

'Yes, that's right,' said Ian.

'Would you allow me to make a suggestion? Our children and grandchildren were going to visit, but the snow has prevented them from coming. Would you and your friends consider spending Christmas Day with us?'

Barbara turned to Ian. Should they? But the Doctor
spoke first. 'Oh, you two can do what you like. But Vicki and
I will return to the –'

Vicki jumped in. 'No! I want to spend a *proper* Christmas
with Ian and Barbara.'

'Please, Doctor,' said Barbara. 'Christmas is a time for
family. And, whether you like it or not, we have become a
family, of sorts.'

'Oh, very well, very well.' The Doctor sounded grumpy,
but there seemed to be a smile hiding in there somewhere.

'Thank you,' said Barbara to the elderly woman. 'If
you're sure we wouldn't be inconveniencing you . . .'

'We would be very glad of the company,' came the warm
reply.

So they set off through the snow, the elderly couple –
Mr and Mrs Robinson – leading the way, the four travellers
following in their footprints. Their destination was a cottage,
as cosy and welcoming as any Barbara had ever known.
Inside, a fire burned in the grate, and a small fir tree sat
nearby, just waiting to be transformed. Something about
the living room struck Barbara as momentarily odd, but
she quickly put it to the back of her mind as Mrs Robinson
handed her a glass of mulled wine. Meanwhile, Vicki and

Ian helped Mr Robinson to decorate the tree. 'We had been wondering whether to bother,' he told them. 'Well, you do it for the kiddies, mainly, don't you?'

Vicki began making yard after yard of paper chains. 'Can we hang up stockings later, please?' she asked.

Barbara opened her mouth to say no, but Mr Robinson gave her a wink and a little nod of the head. 'Oh, I think that could be arranged, young lady,' he said, and Barbara smiled at him in gratitude.

While Barbara and Mrs Robinson played a friendly game of chess, Vicki took off one of her own knee-high socks and attached it to the mantelpiece with a drawing pin. She made Barbara and Ian follow suit, which they did with much laughter and joking. The Doctor refused to participate, so Vicki took off her other sock and pinned it up too. 'That can be yours,' she told the Doctor, who made a *tsch* sound but didn't protest further.

Later, Barbara went to find Mrs Robinson, who was in the kitchen. 'Is there anything I can help with?' she asked.

'No, thank you, my dear,' said the older woman. 'Time for us all to turn in, I think.'

'There is just one more thing,' said Barbara. 'Could I possibly borrow a needle and thread from you?'

'Of course, my dear,' Mrs Robinson replied with a smile and directed her towards her sewing kit.

The cottage was roomier than it had seemed at first; the time travellers were given a bedroom each. Barbara did not go straight to bed. There was something she needed to do first.

She'd just finished her task when she heard the noise. She held her breath for a moment, waiting to see if it came again. It did. Someone was moving around downstairs. But who? The stairs had creaked loudly when everyone had come up to bed, and she'd been awake ever since; she'd have heard if any of the house's other five occupants had ventured from their room.

She slipped on her shoes and opened her door slowly and softly. Even treading as warily as possible, the stairs creaked beneath her feet.

Carefully, so carefully, she pushed open the living-room door. The fire had died down to glowing embers, but there was light enough to see the figure standing beside the mantelpiece. A figure in robes of red, trimmed with white.

Barbara laughed with relief. Mr Robinson – or perhaps even the Doctor – playing Santa Claus. Making it a proper Christmas for Vicki: treats in their waiting stockings.

At the sound, the man turned towards her.

Barbara almost cried out, but it caught in her throat. She barely made a noise as she slid unconscious to the ground.

'Barbara! Barbara! Wake up!'

Barbara heard the voice and obeyed, dragging herself back to consciousness. She was in bed, an ugly candlewick bedspread covering her. Something didn't seem right. Was it because she was so used to waking up in the TARDIS? No, that wasn't it. It was something else. Something she just couldn't put her finger on. And there was no time to think about it, because Vicki was still saying 'Wake up! Wake up!' and sounding so excited.

'Come on, sleepy head! It's Christmas Day! A proper old Earth Christmas Day! And Ian says I'm not allowed to look in my stocking until you come down!'

Barbara followed Vicki downstairs. Everyone else was already there. The socks on the mantelpiece were lumpy and bumpy, empty no longer. Vicki dived for hers, pulling out each small item as though it was the most precious treasure. 'An orange! And look, what are these? Walnuts? And an apple! And a tiny little teddy bear. What have you got, Barbara?'

Smiling, Barbara liberated her own stocking. She reached in and pulled out a small white paper bag. She opened it. 'Oh!' she said. 'It's barley sugar!' Then everything came flooding back. 'It was my father,' she said, turning to the only man she'd ever met who was as brave and strong as her father had been. 'Oh, Ian, I saw my father last night! He was here!'

Ian put an arm round Barbara's shoulder and led her to the uncomfortable horsehair-stuffed sofa. Vicki was looking confused. 'But you said Santa was always your mum or dad,' she said, after Barbara had explained.

'Yes, Vicki, I know. But my father died in the war. He couldn't have been here, in 1963.' She turned to Mrs Robinson. 'This is 1963, isn't it?'

The old lady nodded. 'Of course it is, dear. I think you must have been having a bad dream.'

'Here, take this.' Mr Robinson had vanished into the kitchen, and now returned with a glass of brandy. 'Drink it all down, now. Don't worry, there's still plenty left for the pudding.'

'And for the snapdragon?' asked Vicki.

'Yes, and for that too.'

Barbara drank the brandy, and tried to tell herself it made her feel better. Of course it had been a dream. Of course she hadn't really seen her long-dead, much-loved father.

But at the back of her mind she heard the Doctor's words from the previous night: *Don't lose sight of the idea that this may be a trap!*

When Vicki was out of earshot, she pulled the Doctor over to one side. 'I was thinking about what you were saying,' she told him, quietly. 'About it being such a coincidence we landed on this planet at this time. About how it might be a trap.'

'Oh, no no no,' said the Doctor, waving her worries aside. 'No, I spoke rashly. Forget everything I said and concentrate on having a happy Christmas.'

If the Doctor – as suspicious and sceptical as he was – thought things were fine, well, they probably were. Barbara tried to do as he said. She would enjoy Christmas Day.

Barbara offered once again to help Mrs Robinson in the kitchen, and was once more refused. 'There's so little to do,' Mrs Robinson said, which was the exact opposite of what Barbara's mother used to say every year at this time as she tried to juggle turkey and trimmings and pudding and brandy butter and all the many things that made up a traditional Christmas dinner.

The reason for Mrs Robinson's attitude became clear when they sat down at the table and she produced the pudding. That was it. Just a pudding. No turkey, no stuffing, no Yorkshire puddings or sprouts. One pudding, soft blue flames flickering around it.

Ian and Barbara exchanged a look. 'Not even custard!' mouthed Ian silently, and Barbara shrugged in sympathy. No one else seemed to realise there was anything out of the ordinary.

Mr Robinson cut the pudding into six equal slices and bowls were passed round the table.

'Oh!' cried Ian, taking a mouthful. 'I think I've got the sixpence!' He removed the coin from his mouth and polished it clean with a napkin.

Barbara leaned over to look. 'It's got Queen Victoria's head on it! It's a proper old silver sixpence, just like the one we used at home.'

Ian turned the coin over in his hand. 'Not quite like the one you had at home, I suspect.'

Barbara looked at it again. 'It looks the same to me.'

'Keep looking.' He turned the coin over again. Now his meaning became obvious.

'Oh! It's a two-headed coin! How funny.'

'Can we pull the crackers now?' asked Vicki. Ian put the coin down as the colourful red-and-green crackers were handed out. Barbara took one and held it out to the Doctor. He pulled.

They were both knocked backwards by the explosion. As the Doctor staggered to his feet, eyebrows singed and face blackened, Barbara fought to keep down hysterical laughter.

'I think,' said the Doctor, with as much dignity as he could muster, 'that the makers may have rather overdone the gunpowder. I suggest we forgo the rest of them.'

'Anyway, it's time for the queen's speech,' said Mr Robinson. 'Everyone gather round!'

They all squashed together on the sofa, waiting for the tiny television set to warm up. Eventually a face began to take shape. Barbara stared at the blurry form. Once again, she had the distinct feeling that something was wrong. As the image became clearer, so did her thoughts. 'But . . . that's not the queen!' she cried out.

The Robinsons looked puzzled. 'Of course that's the queen,' said Mr Robinson. 'She looks just like she looks on the sixpence.'

'Exactly!' said Barbara. 'That's Queen Victoria! It should be Queen Elizabeth!'

'Just a bit of . . . time slippage,' said the Doctor. 'Nothing to worry about. Nothing at all.'

Vicki jumped up. 'Let's do presents. That'll make everything better.' She ran over to the living-room door and opened it wide. 'Come on!' she called.

Heavy footprints approached. Barbara looked on in horror as a giant crashed through the door. A thing out of a terrible nightmare – no, not out of a nightmare, out of a horror film . . .

'No! Can't you all see how wrong this is?' she cried. 'The Doctor was right. It is a trap! We have to get away!'

'No, not yet!' pleaded Vicki. 'There's still the snapdragon!'

Barbara was almost unsurprised to see a dragon fly through the window, a dragon wreathed in blue flame, dropping almonds and raisins as it went. She grabbed hold of Vicki with one hand and Ian with the other, trying to drag them away.

The dragon breathed fire, and the cottage began to burn. But there was no warmth from the flames. Mr and Mrs Robinson were burning too, but still smiling, unconcerned.

'All right, then, games!' said Vicki anxiously. 'Blind man's buff! Come on, Barbara, you be it!'

The world suddenly went dark.

'I can't see!' exclaimed Barbara. 'I can't see! Please! Ian! Vicki! Doctor! We have to get out of here!' But their hands slipped from hers as she lurched forward, desperate, scared, determined . . .

. . . and then suddenly able to see again.

She was in the TARDIS, on her bed. She'd never left her bed.

'Not a dream,' she said aloud. 'It was too real to be a dream.'

A muffled sob from the other bed. 'I'm so sorry!' cried Vicki.

There was a knock on the door. 'Are you decent?' called Ian. He and the Doctor came in.

The Doctor put an arm round Vicki's shoulders. 'Don't cry, child. You meant it for the best.'

'You know?' said Vicki sadly, quietly.

'Not at first. But I worked it out. Oh, you silly girl!'

'Explain,' demanded a confused Barbara. 'Will someone please explain!'

'It was meant to be my Christmas present to you,' said Vicki. 'When we got the minerals to run the Doctor's machine, I decided to try it. I wanted to give you the Christmas you wished for. But I think I might have got some elements wrong.'

'Like exploding crackers and a real snapping dragon instead of the Victorian parlour game?' said Ian. 'No, it wasn't a fully accurate representation of England in 1963. And what was that giant who crashed through the door?'

'Oh, did I get that wrong too? I thought that was one of the gifts you traditionally gave at Christmas: gold, Frankenstein and myrrh.'

Ian raised his eyes to the ceiling. 'Frankincense – *not* Frankenstein! What do they teach you at school?'

'What was the machine, Doctor?' asked Barbara. 'What does it do?'

'It creates a shared dream,' the Doctor replied, 'which can be shaped by the operator to help those recovering from mental trauma to heal.'

'I think it's caused more trauma than it's healed,' began Barbara, but when she saw Vicki's tragic expression she changed what she had been about to say. 'But it was a very kind thought, Vicki. We have a saying in our time: "It's the thought that counts". Thank you.'

'Well, let's see where we've landed,' the Doctor said. 'Come along, child.' He left, and Vicki followed. Ian and Barbara were alone.

'She meant well,' Ian said after a short silence.

'I know she did. I'm not angry. It was just . . . seeing my father again,' Barbara said as a tear ran down her cheek. She reached into a pocket for a handkerchief. 'Oh!'

Barbara held out the thing she'd found. A man's large white handkerchief with a monogram in one corner: the initials *I. C.* 'It was to be my Christmas present to you,' she said. 'I borrowed a needle and thread from Mrs Robinson and embroidered it. But how on earth did it get in my pocket? It was only a dream.'

'I don't know, but I'm glad it did. Thank you.' Ian took it from her, smiled and put it in his own pocket. Then he too looked puzzled as he held out his palm to show what he'd found there.

'The silver sixpence! From the pudding!' Barbara exclaimed.

Ian nodded. 'The sixpence that brings luck to the one who finds it. Maybe it's a sign that we will soon be home after all.'

Barbara smiled. 'Yes, perhaps we will. But I already count myself lucky. Lucky to have such good friends.' She leaned forward and kissed Ian on the cheek. 'Happy Christmas, Ian – whatever day it may be.'

A COMEDY
OF TERRORS

Written by Colin Brake

Illustrated by Melissa Castrillón

'Doctor, could you no' have landed the TARDIS somewhere friendly for a change?' said the handsome young Scot dressed in a grey turtleneck and a tartan kilt. A much smaller, elfin-faced girl with her dark hair in a neat bob stood beside him. Both had their hands held up in a gesture of surrender. A third figure stumbled through the doors of the TARDIS behind them, to join them in the brightly lit spaceship corridor. He was a man of indeterminate age in a battered frock coat and shapeless chequered trousers.

'Oh dear,' the Doctor muttered as soon as he saw what was going on. A uniformed official stood in their path, accompanied by a pair of armed guards, whose weapons were pointed directly at them. The Doctor copied his friends and raised his hands in the air, palms facing out.

'This is a secure area,' stated the official. 'Who are you, and how did you get in here?'

A metallic badge on his chest labelled him Security Commander Barwell.

'Well, er, Commander Barwell,' the Doctor began, thinking as fast as he could. 'As a matter of fact, we are –'

'With me, of course,' said a new voice from further down the corridor.

The guards stood aside as the speaker joined them. She was a tall humanoid, with a wide face and a wide body to match. She wore a bright red jacket, yellow trousers and a blue-and-white striped shirt. Zoe thought she looked like someone who had got dressed in the dark.

'Mrs Butlins?' Commander Barwell asked.

'They're obviously the actors I sent for from the agency,' explained the woman, beaming.

'I see, madam. In that case, we will bid you good day as we have duties to perform,' replied the commander, and he left, taking the guards with him.

'I'm Billie Butlins,' said the woman, firmly shaking hands with the Doctor, Zoe and Jamie. 'No doubt you were told to report to me? You *are* the agency actors, I presume? I wasn't expecting you quite so soon but it's no bad thing you are here.

It will give you more time to study the scripts.'

'Agency actors? Scripts?' said Jamie, looking confused.

'We prefer the term "performers",' the Doctor said quickly, speaking over him.

'Excellent!' The woman's smile widened. 'We are a small company, and we all need to be multitalented if we're to pull off this performance.'

'Performance?' Zoe looked equally puzzled.

'Didn't the agency tell you? In honour of the festive season,' Mrs Butlins continued, 'and to mark Princess Triana's visit to the planet Luxona, we will present Mr William Shakespeare's classic pantomime *Much Ado About a Beanstalk*!' Then, as if to punctuate her grand announcement, she broke wind.

Jamie wafted a hand in front of his nose as an awful smell filled the air.

'We can't wait,' muttered the Doctor, coughing slightly.

'Here are your scripts.' Mrs Butlins reached into a handbag and produced one for each of them. As she handed them out she let off another foul-smelling trump.

'What's with all the farts?' muttered Jamie.

'What's that?' asked Mrs Butlins sharply.

'Parts, Mrs Butlins,' the Doctor interjected. 'My friend Jamie was wondering which parts he might get.'

'You're professionals. I'm sure you can sort that out amongst yourselves. We'll rehearse when we reach Luxona,' said Mrs Butlins, walking off.

Jamie glared at the Doctor. 'Actors?' he complained. 'What have you got us into now, Doctor?'

'Well, Jamie, I'm not entirely sure,' the Doctor confessed. He rubbed his hands together, thinking carefully. 'But something doesn't smell right about Mrs Butlins.'

'You can say that again!' exclaimed Zoe with a giggle.

Once inside the rooms that they had been assigned, the Doctor used his sonic screwdriver to access the ship's computer to find out where they were. The TARDIS had landed on board the Royal Space Cruiser *Starlight*, which was taking Princess Triana of the Sita Federation and her stepmother, the Queen-Regent, on an official Christmas visit to the planet Luxona. He couldn't spot anything obviously amiss but there was something nagging him about the less-than-fragrant Mrs Butlins and the Doctor wanted to know what it was. He decided to investigate.

Meanwhile, Zoe decided to explore the ship and found her way to the observation gallery, a small room accessed by a staircase so steep that it was almost a ladder. It had a number of seats set out beneath a thick, transparent domed ceiling through which the stars could be seen as the ship hurtled through interstellar space. Zoe always enjoyed such views – she liked the challenge of trying to calculate how many stars were visible and how far away they were from each other. One thing she regretted about travel by TARDIS was the lack of portholes.

'Beautiful, isn't it?' said a voice behind her.

Zoe turned and saw that she had been joined by a tall, elegant teenager in a regal blue gown with an ermine trim. *She must be the princess who Mrs Butlins mentioned*, thought Zoe, quickly rising to her feet.

'Your Highness,' she began, attempting a curtsey.

'Please don't,' said the princess. 'Just call me Triana.'

Zoe introduced herself, keeping to the actor cover story; to her dismay, the princess was fascinated. Zoe did her best to answer the princess's many questions in character.

Within minutes, Zoe could tell that the princess was lonely and lacked friends her own age. Triana explained that she led a relatively solitary life, devoted to duty. Her mother had died in childbirth, and her father, King Urdrageth, had soon remarried. When Triana was five, her father was killed when he fell from his horse on a hunting trip and his second wife, Lady Vaxene, had become Queen-Regent. Since then, every waking moment had been spent preparing Triana for the day when she would become queen on her eighteenth birthday.

'And when do you turn eighteen?' asked Zoe.

'That's just it. I had my eighteenth birthday six months ago.'

'Yet your stepmother still rules as Queen-Regent?'

Triana nodded, the silver-and-gold coronet in her hair glistening as it caught the light. 'There has been a small technicality that has delayed my coronation. The Sita Federation is a union of five planets across two neighbouring star systems, all under the rule of our family. I should have been born on my family's home planet of Sita Major,' she told Zoe, 'but my mother went into labour early, while she and my father were on Luxona dealing with a miners' strike. I need the official records of my birth from the hospital on Luxona to ratify my coronation.'

'And that's what we are travelling to collect?' Zoe asked.

'That and, just as importantly, the other half of this.' She showed Zoe a pendant that hung on a chain round her neck.

Looking at it more closely, Zoe could see that the pendant was a bubble made of some kind of clear material that contained half of a silver ring.

'My father's royal seal,' Triana explained. 'The ring has

been handed down through the generations of my family. It is a symbol of our royal authority.'

'But why is there only half of it?'

'When I was born my father ordered his ring to be cut in half, and had one half placed in this pendant as a gift to me.'

'And his half?'

'In a matching pendant, which he wore from that day on, until he died.'

'I'm sorry,' said Zoe.

'Don't be. I hardly knew him. And, from what I've heard, I'm not sure I would have liked him. After the Luxonian rebellion twenty-five years ago, he made them pay a terrible price. When – *if* – I become queen, I hope to make things better for the people of Luxona.'

'So what happened to his pendant?'

'It was lost when he died. But it's recently been found again and handed in to the authorities. The Luxonian people will present it to me as a Christmas gift, and after my coronation I will lift the taxes that have forced them to ravage their beautiful planet through strip-mining.'

Jamie had been given the task of spying on the Queen-Regent. He found her in the spaceship's main lounge. Taking a seat close to her position, Jamie pretended to read his script, while listening carefully to what was being discussed.

The Lady Vaxene was a tall, thin woman, dressed in a stylish but practical two-piece suit. She had watchful, deep blue eyes, thin lips and high cheekbones. One of her retinue, a terrified-looking man with sweat beading his forehead and a slight twitch in one eye, approached her nervously.

'My lady,' began the man. 'There is news from Luxona.'

Vaxene fixed him with her steely gaze. 'What news?' she asked.

'It's reported that the birth records and the other half of your late husband's ring have been . . . mislaid,' he stammered.

Jamie felt sorry for the man; it was clear he was expecting the Queen-Regent to be furious. To Jamie's surprise, however, Vaxene didn't seem particularly concerned.

'And?' she said dismissively.

'Unfortunately, ma'am, there are many on Luxona who remember the rule of your late husband with . . . little affection,' continued the man. 'They may be behind this theft.'

'There are many on Luxona who bear no love for us,' Vaxene said simply.

'Indeed. They claim the mining operations ordered in the aftermath of the rebellion have taken a high toll on the Luxonian ecosystem.'

'They paid the price for their disloyalty,' said Vaxene coolly.

'For twenty years,' the man added under his breath.

'Tell Commander Barwell to double his patrols and to be prepared for a hostile reception,' ordered Vaxene. 'And have someone inform my stepdaughter that there might yet be a further delay before she can become queen.'

The messenger bowed formally, almost scraping his head on the floor, before righting himself and hurrying away. Jamie watched him go before he realised with a shock that the Queen-Regent was also now on her feet and walking directly towards him. Quickly he turned his eyes to his script. Suddenly the pages were pulled out of his hand, turned upside down, then thrust back at him.

'I always find it easier to read when the words are the right way up,' said Vaxene, as she walked away. 'Don't you?'

The Doctor had located Billie Butlins' cabin. Checking that he wasn't being watched, he used his sonic to open the door, then slipped inside. He began to search the room, but had hardly started when suddenly the door flew open and the enormous bulk of the director filled the door frame.

'Ah, *there* you are,' said the Doctor, thinking on his feet. 'I wondered where you'd got to.'

'How did you get in here?' demanded Mrs Butlins suspiciously.

'The door was open,' replied the Doctor. 'You must have left it ajar when you went out.'

Ignoring the frown that threatened to split Mrs Butlins' forehead, the Doctor went on. 'I wanted to speak to you about . . .' The Doctor racked his brains desperately, then inspiration hit him. 'About the script!'

'The script?'

'It's a delight!' exclaimed the Doctor. 'I take it the adaptation is your own?'

'Why, yes,' said Mrs Butlins, clearly flattered.

'I know they say you can't improve on Shakespeare, but, like I said to young William once, there's always another draft to be had.'

'You met Shakespeare?' said the director, looking puzzled.

'Once or twice,' the Doctor replied.

'How exciting!' Mrs Butlins said, clearly impressed.

'Actually, I helped him out with some of his plays,' said the Doctor with mock modesty.

'Really? Which ones?' Mrs Butlins asked.

The Doctor feigned a poor memory. 'Well, there was that one set in Scotland. With the three witches . . .'

'*Macbeth!* You must mean the tragedy of Macbeth.'

'Yes, that's the one.' The Doctor looked carefully at Mrs
Butlins, a hint of triumph in his eyes. 'But we can't stand
around chatting shop all day, can we? I've got lines to learn
. . . See you later.' With that the Doctor skipped round the
bulky director and out of the door. As he left he heard the
unmistakable sound of more wind being broken.

'So I have to dress up as a boy, and you dress up as a woman?'
Zoe was finding it hard to get her head around the peculiar
traditions of pantomime.

'Yes, Zoe,' the Doctor explained patiently. 'You play the
Principal Boy. Traditionally, the lead male role in the panto is
played by a female actor.'

'But the Dame is played by a man?' Zoe said sceptically.

'Oh yes! The Dame is a very specific role in pantomime.
Some of the finest comedians in theatrical history have played
a Dame,' the Doctor told his companions.

'Aye, well, you're always making us laugh,' Jamie
retorted. 'So I'm sure you'll make a great Dame.'

'And are you happy about your role, Jamie?' asked Zoe,
trying her best to stifle a grin.

Unlike the Doctor and Zoe, Jamie was not enjoying
being an actor. Changing the subject, he asked the others how
they had got on with their investigations.

The Doctor listed his misgivings about the mysterious Billie Butlins: firstly, there was her name, which sounded suspiciously like a pseudonym; secondly, there was her failure to react when the Doctor had talked about meeting a playwright who had lived over a thousand years in the past; and, finally, there was the matter of her saying the name of 'the Scottish Play' aloud.

'I don't understand,' said Zoe.

The Doctor explained that, although over the centuries there were lots of things that became forgotten or confused about William Shakespeare, there was one thing that was never lost: those in the theatre were always deeply superstitious about mentioning the play *Macbeth*'s name, and never referred to it as anything but the Scottish Play.

'So, three strikes against our Mrs Butlins,' declared the Doctor. 'And maybe a fourth – those foul and frequent farts!'

'But you cannae think her a wrong 'un just because the lady farts like a Redcoat?'

'No, Jamie, ordinarily I wouldn't, but the other evidence is very strong.'

Zoe told the Doctor and Jamie about her conversation with the princess. The Doctor nodded, carefully adding the new information to everything else they had learned so far.

'The key is this pendant with the ring fragment inside it,'

the Doctor said, after musing for a while. 'Clearly it was on Luxona all these years and recently surfaced.'

'But now it's gone again,' said Jamie, recalling the discussion he had eavesdropped on.

'Conveniently just when it was about to be presented to Triana,' added the Doctor.

'But Triana will be a friend to Luxona,' Zoe pointed out. 'It's not in the interests of the Luxonians to delay her coronation.'

The Doctor nodded. 'So, who *would* benefit, then?'

'I can think of one person,' Jamie said. 'Her stepmother!'

The capital of Luxona was a city called New Manchester, which looked very much like a nineteenth-century European city – brick-built houses, cobbled streets, municipal squares and public parks.

Zoe was amused to see that festive celebrations were in full swing. Christmas trees sparkling with tinsel and candles stood in most windows, and garlands of holly decorated many front doors. The Doctor reminded his companions how many areas of Earth had been settled by people of various cultures who, even when they had lived there for many generations, still held on to the traditions of their forebears. The same was apparently true of Luxona. Riding in an open-topped carriage pulled by what appeared to be unicorns, the three space–time travellers soon pulled up in front of a magnificent theatre.

'A Victorian playhouse,' murmured the Doctor. 'How splendid!'

The view inside the building was even more spectacular than the exterior. The auditorium resembled a palace, with a rich red carpet, seats of polished walnut and plush purple cushions, and ornate gold statues on the walls. Despite the extravagant setting, theatre-goers could not help but focus their attention on the stage itself, framed like a picture by its proscenium arch and lit by a complex collection of hanging lanterns and spotlights.

Although Billie Butlins had hired a trio of leading actors from Sita Major, the rest of the cast was made up of locals, and a stage crew had already been working hard for some time. Under Billie's slightly erratic direction, rehearsals were soon under way.

As they worked through the script – which seemed to be a number of different traditional pantomimes mangled together – the Doctor noticed that they had acquired an audience. The Lady Vaxene, accompanied by her small retinue, watched a comic routine between Zoe and Jamie that ended with the former pouring a bucket of cold water over the latter. The slapstick performance failed to raise so much as a smile on Vaxene's face. Billie Butlins called for the company to 'take five', then hurried across to assure the royal visitor that the final show would be much funnier.

Jamie sat down towards the back of the stage and started drying his hair with a towel. Suddenly there was a loud crack and he was aware of something dark hurtling towards him from above. Instinctively he threw himself forward and, using the natural rake of the stage, rolled towards the footlights at the front of it. Behind him, one of the large overhead lamps crashed on to the stage, smashing into thousands of pieces. The point of impact was the exact spot where Jamie had been sitting just moments ago!

With the rehearsal adjourned, the Doctor, Jamie and Zoe retreated to the dressing room. 'How could an accident like that just happen?' asked Zoe as she cleaned up a cut on Jamie's arm.

'I'm very much afraid that it wasn't an accident,' the Doctor told them.

'What do you mean?' demanded Jamie.

'That sound you heard – just before the lamp fell – that was a gunshot. I took a look at the rope that secured the lamp, and it had been shot clean through.'

'Somebody tried to kill me?' Jamie was horrified. 'But who? Why?'

'I've an idea about the first. I saw one of the Queen-Regent's servants going backstage just before the accident,' the Doctor told them.

Suddenly the door opened and an enormous shadow fell over them.

'The show must go on!' thundered Billie Butlins.

It was time to get back to rehearsal.

'How do I look?' asked the Doctor a few hours later, smoothing down his costume in readiness for the final performance.

Zoe and Jamie exchanged a glance. The Doctor was wearing a ridiculous blonde wig, make-up and a long ballgown stuffed with balloons to make him look vaguely female.

'Beautiful,' lied Zoe. She was dressed in a princely tunic with blue knee-high boots.

Jamie thought that perhaps he was the luckiest of the three. His main role was as Palace Cook, and he had a simple costume of a chef's white tunic, chequered black-and-white trousers and a tall chef's hat, which the Doctor was eyeing jealously.

'I should like a hat like that,' he muttered to himself.

Billie Butlins hurried past. 'Opening positions,' she announced. 'Curtains up in five minutes. Break a leg, everyone!'

'That didn't sound very friendly,' said Jamie indignantly, as the large woman disappeared into the wings.

'It's a traditional way of wishing a performer luck in the theatre,' the Doctor explained.

'Och, there's that stench again,' complained Jamie, waving a hand under his nose.

'It's the wrong kind of smell for wind,' said Zoe, frowning. 'It's more like . . . well, bad breath.'

The Doctor suddenly clapped his hands together. 'Of course, it all makes sense now!'

Zoe and Jamie looked at him incredulously. 'It does?'

'Listen,' whispered the Doctor. 'We need to be prepared.'

The Doctor, who was playing one of the Ugly Sisters, performed a scene in which he forced the poor Palace Cook, acted by Jamie, to get messier and messier as he tried to meet the sister's increasingly impossible demands. The audience loved it, and the Doctor noted that even the Queen-Regent, seated in the Royal Box with the princess, was laughing.

Could she really be planning to steal the crown from her

stepdaughter? the Doctor wondered.

The scene completed, the performers made their exits: Jamie to one side of the stage, and the Doctor into the wings on the other side.

The production's costume supervisor, a cheerful blue Luxonian called Maynard, was there to meet the Doctor, who had a costume change before his next scene. However, instead of handing the Doctor his new dress, Maynard looked around nervously, then beckoned the Doctor into an alcove.

'I need to show you something,' he began, then stopped himself, seeing someone over the Doctor's shoulder. The Doctor turned and saw Billie Butlins in the opposite wings, watching them carefully.

'Can't speak here,' muttered Maynard. 'Meet me in your dressing room at the interval. I'll explain everything. But hold on to this – for safe keeping.' The Luxonian pressed something into the Doctor's hand and hurried off.

The Doctor looked down and saw that he had been given a golden egg, one of the props that featured in the finale of the show. He popped it in his pocket.

Twenty minutes later, the curtain came down for the interval. The Doctor found Zoe and Jamie and told them about his mysterious encounter with Maynard. 'Hopefully he can explain everything,' said the Doctor as he opened his dressing-room door.

Inside, though, they found the poor Luxonian lying prone on the floor, with Billie Butlins standing over him. Billie turned towards them, her face a picture of anger.

'When I say "run" –' began the Doctor.

'We know the drill,' said Jamie, cutting him short. Not taking their eyes off the director, the trio started to back towards the door.

'What's she doing?' asked Zoe.

Billie Butlins had reached up to her forehead. She then began to unzip it. A shaft of light burst from a slit that opened up under her hairline and, impossibly, a massive orange alien with jet-black eyes emerged from within the human skin of Billie Butlins.

'Ah, it's as I guessed. She's a Raxacoricofallapatorian!' said the Doctor.

'A what?' asked Jamie.

'I'll tell you later,' replied the Doctor, yanking off the pantomime dress so it wouldn't impede his escape. '*Run!*'

They ran. The terrifying orange monster lumbered after them, moving with surprising speed for a creature of its size.

The three skidded on to the stage just as the curtain was rising for the final act. They came to a halt, slightly surprised to find the audience clapping their arrival. They looked for their pursuer but there was no sign of the alien.

'We're being chased,' Zoe told the audience. 'Has anyone seen a great big orange alien?'

'It's behind you!' shouted someone in the crowd, thinking this was part of the show.

Jamie spun round, but there was no one there.

'No, it's behind *you*, princess!' shouted the Doctor, pointing towards the Royal Box. The alien had just appeared at the back of the box, one claw pointing directly at Princess Triana.

'Be careful!' warned the Doctor. 'She may have poisoned darts in her claws.'

But even as he spoke something shot out of the end of the alien's claw. Before anyone else could move, the Queen-Regent had thrown herself in front of her stepdaughter.

Jamie was already using the carved decorations and drapes to climb up to the balcony. As he dropped into the Royal Box, he found the alien gone and Vaxene lying in the arms of her stepdaughter.

'She saved my life,' said Triana in disbelief.

'Please, protect the princess,' whispered Vaxene, her eyelids fluttering.

'We will,' promised Jamie, then added, 'I'm very sorry

that we ever doubted you.'

Down on the stage, the orange monster suddenly reappeared before the Doctor and Zoe.

'You've ruined my plans!' screamed the alien. 'I shall rip everyone in this theatre apart, Doctor, starting with you!'

'Not under my watch, you won't.' The Doctor turned to his companion. 'Time for the custard pies, Zoe!'

Zoe nodded and rushed into the wings, where she picked up two paper plates piled high with what looked like shaving foam.

She passed one to the Doctor, and they simultaneously threw them at the alien. The effect was immediate. The alien exploded in a disgusting, gooey mess!

The audience rose to their feet, clapping and cheering at what they thought was a very clever stage illusion. The Doctor, however, looked horrified.

'I was hoping the custard tarts would incapacitate her, not make her explode!' the Doctor said regretfully, wiping the alien slime from his face.

'She would have killed everyone on board, Doctor,' Zoe said, patting his arm. 'Thank goodness that hunch of yours did the trick, as I'm not sure how else we would have stopped her.'

'I suppose so . . .' replied the Doctor, but he still looked troubled. 'Talking of tricks, I have a final one right here.'

He pulled the golden egg he had been given earlier from his pocket and banged it on the stage, cracking it open. From within, he extracted a familiar-looking pendant. 'I think *this* is what everyone has been looking for.'

The celebrations went on for days. The Doctor, Jamie and Zoe were hailed as heroes. Happily, a Luxonian doctor had miraculously found an antidote to the Raxacoricofallapatorian's poison and Lady Vaxene was recovering in a local hospital.

Triana had kept her promise and, in her first act as queen, she released Luxona from its obligations to pay the extortionate tax demanded by her late father. The Doctor had established that the companies responsible for the violent strip-mining of Luxona's natural beauty were funded by a Raxacoricofallapatorian family named Hanazeen-Blathereen, who had profited handsomely from the mining operations for decades. The companies had already abandoned their equipment and left the planet.

'When did you realise Billie Butlins was an alien?' the new queen asked the three travellers during a private audience.

The Doctor put his hands together and tried to look

modest. 'Well, I had my suspicions from the moment I met her. The name she chose was not particularly convincing. And then there were the gaps in her stage knowledge. And, of course, there was the matter of her malodorous gaseous eruptions.'

The queen looked confused.

'Her smelly farts,' explained Jamie helpfully.

'Which I said smelled more like bad breath,' added Zoe.

'Which made me think of calcium-based lifeforms,' the Doctor concluded. 'Like those from Raxacoricofallapatorius.'

'Say again?' the queen said.

'I'd rather not, if you don't mind, Your Majesty. It's a bit of a mouthful. Now, I knew that the inhabitants from that world are dangerous hunters when in their natural form, but they have a weakness – acetic acid.'

'So we prepared some special custard pies laced with vinegar,' said Zoe.

The Doctor looked grave. 'Unfortunately, we rather overdid it. I really didn't intend to blow her up.'

'In doing so, you saved the lives of everyone on board,' said the queen. 'We are eternally grateful. You will stay for the Grand Christmas Ball tonight?'

It was more an instruction than a question. Zoe and Jamie looked at each other. A bit of a knees-up sounded like a nice idea. The Doctor, however, didn't look so keen.

'Perhaps you can perform a little skit for us, as well?' added the queen hopefully.

'Of course. We'd be honoured,' said the Doctor. 'We just need to pop back to collect some props from our special blue box.'

'I had that brought here from the ship,' Queen Triana told them. 'It's in the adjacent room.' She nodded at an attendant, who opened a door to reveal the TARDIS.

'Ah, excellent,' said the Doctor. 'Come on then, Zoe, Jamie. Lend a hand.'

Realising what was about to happen, Zoe and Jamie hurried after the Doctor, who was already unlocking the TARDIS door. Zoe gave a little wave to the queen as she darted inside.

A moment later, the TARDIS doors closed behind them. A creaking, groaning sound filled the air. To the queen's astonishment, the blue box began to fade from existence. After a few seconds, it had vanished completely.

'Well!' declared the queen. 'I'm not sure if the Doctor and his friends were actors after all, but they certainly know how to put on a good show!'

THE CHRISTMAS
INVERSION

Written by Jacqueline Rayner

Illustrated by Sara Gianassi

'Help us . . . Please, Doctor. Help . . . us . . .'
Jo looked frantically around the TARDIS control room. Where was the voice coming from? It was a female voice, and sounded calm despite the panic her words implied – but it wasn't a voice that Jo recognised. She ran to the main doors and called into the Doctor's workshop. 'Doctor! Hurry, please!'

The Doctor appeared, followed by a young man in a khaki uniform with three pips on each shoulder. The uniformed man was carrying a bizarre device – well, Jo assumed it was a device of some sort, rather than just a few armfuls of assorted junk. There were spoons involved, and coils of wire, half a transistor radio and, strangest of all, a tennis racquet that had seen better days.

'Just over there, Mike,' the Doctor said, gesturing to the floor by the central control console.

Captain Mike Yates did as he was told, then turned away with a cheery wave. 'Catch you later,' he said. 'Don't want to be dragged off to visit the dinosaurs or Tutankhamun or something.'

'Nice boy, Tutankhamun,' said the Doctor. 'Didn't like it if I beat him at Senet, though.'

Mike shot a look at Jo as he exited and she giggled, but the Doctor called her attention back to the problem at hand. 'Any change?' he asked.

She shook her head. 'She's still saying the same thing over and over again. But I think I've made out a few more words. She says "request" at one point, and "desperate".'

The Doctor unspooled wire from either end of his device, attaching one end to the scanner screen high on one wall, and the other to a control panel. 'Let's see if we can get a clearer signal.'

The spoons started to vibrate, clattering against each other. The tennis racquet began to swing backwards and forwards like a metronome. A picture formed on the scanner. It showed a woman, middle-aged, serious. There was a Christmas tree behind her. As the picture became clearer, so did her words.

'I have one request. Doctor, if you're out there, we need you. I don't know what to do. If you can hear me, Doctor. If anyone knows the Doctor, if anyone can find him. The situation has never been more desperate. Help us. Please, Doctor. Help us.'

The Doctor and Jo watched in silence until the message began to repeat. 'I have one request . . .'

'We have to help her!' said Jo. 'Unless . . .' She paused. 'What if it's the Master? What if he's gone into the future and hypnotised this woman to send an appeal into the ether to lure you into a terrible trap?'

'I don't think so, Jo,' said the Doctor. 'I can feel a connection, something that's linking me to her – something from my future, or my past.'

'If it's from your past, you'd remember it, wouldn't you?'

'Not necessarily. Apparently I got caught up in that Omega business twice before.' He patted his machine. 'Anyway, we're going to follow the transmission and find out what this is all about. Preparing to follow . . . now!'

The Doctor threw a switch – and, at exactly the same moment, Mike Yates came back through the TARDIS doors, holding out a spoon. 'Doctor, I think this must have dropped off . . .' His words trailed away as he watched the central column rise and fall, while the doors slammed shut of their own accord behind him. 'Your machine,' he finished.

'Ah,' said the Doctor. 'Mike. How do you feel about a little visit to the early twenty-first century?'

By the look on Mike's face, Jo was fairly certain it wasn't a prospect he relished.

A few moments later, the TARDIS landed. The Doctor operated the door controls – then staggered slightly.

'Doctor! Are you all right?' Jo ran to his side.

A thread of gold drifted from his fingers, an airy, insubstantial spider's web, winding its way through the opening doors. 'Energy,' he gasped. 'Time Lord energy . . .'

'The Master!' cried Jo. 'It must be the Master! He's draining your energy so you'll be weakened when he hands the Earth over to some hideous aliens who want to enslave all of humanity!'

The Doctor managed to shake his head weakly. 'No . . . it's me,' he said. 'A future version of me is here, somewhere, and needs regenerative energy. He's taking it from me – strong to weak – energy osmosis.'

The golden thread dissolved and the Doctor stood up straight. 'It's over,' he said. 'He . . . I . . . have what was needed –' He broke off as a blonde woman flew through the TARDIS doors.

She stopped, stood stock still, mouth open wide, words frozen on her lips. The carrier bags she was holding dropped unheeded to the floor, tins of food spilling everywhere.

'Who are you?' she screeched.

'I, madam, am the Doctor.'

'Oh my god, you've done it again,' she said. Then she took in Jo and Mike. 'And you've done it to them too! Oh, Rose! Rose, my precious baby! He's changed your face as well!'

Jo stared, not knowing what to say. 'I'm not –' she began, but the woman wasn't listening.

'At least you've kept your hair the right colour. Might even be a bit prettier. Let me look at you. Yes, I like the nose. But you!' She turned to Mike. 'Mickey, what has he done to you?'

'Er, I prefer Mike.'

'Oh, you've changed that too, have you? Well, Mickey, Mike – it's the same thing. Don't you go giving yourself airs and graces just because you've been raiding the dressing-up box. What are you supposed to be, anyway? A general or something?'

Once more she'd moved on before Mike had finished saying, 'A captain, actually.'

The woman took hold of the sleeve of the Doctor's

velvet jacket. 'And, talking of dressing up, what have you done with Howard's dressing gown? You'll have to buy him a new one if you've lost it, you know.'

The Doctor shook himself free. 'Unhand me, madam!'

'It was a good one, too. Marks and Sparks, not from down the market.' She folded her arms and sniffed dismissively. 'And what's all this "madam" business. This is me, Jackie Tyler, not the Queen of England.'

Jo had been thinking. 'You didn't say it,' she said.

'Say what?' Jackie fired back.

'That it's bigger on the inside than the outside. You didn't even look surprised.'

The woman – Jackie – threw up her hands. 'Well, I was only in here with you all, what, two minutes ago?' Then her face fell. She stared pleadingly at Jo. 'Oh no. Is this one of those things? Like when you thought you'd been gone a day but it was a year for me? Has it been two minutes for me and, I don't know, two months for you? Or two years? Or *twenty* years?'

'Er . . . something like that,' said Mike, looking at Jo rather than Jackie, his eyes clearly saying *I don't know what's going on so we'd better humour her.*

'It's been ages, hasn't it? I mean, you've had time to redecorate.' Jackie looked around. 'I like it. You'll never

be short of washing-up bowls again. And you've got a
new telly too!'

'. . . If you can hear me, Doctor. If anyone knows the
Doctor, if anyone can find him . . .'

'Does it get Freeview, or haven't you got a set-top box?'

'Do you know who this is?' Jo asked, pointing at the
woman on the monitor.

'What, does this facelift thingy wipe your memory too?
That's Harriet Jones! Prime minister! You helped her save the
world! Bring about Britain's Golden Age. You know. *Her!*'

'Golden Age,' echoed Mike. 'Sounds good.'

'Well, it *was* good until this happened – the spaceship
and all the people up on the roof, ready to jump.' She
gestured behind her, to the world outside the TARDIS.
The Doctor walked past her, out of the doors. The others
followed.

All four gazed up. A tower block, a hive of balconies and
broken windows – yes, every single window was broken, how
odd – concrete grime decorated occasionally with garlands of
tinsel. Then up higher. Up to the roof.

'Look at all those people!' gasped Jo. 'What are they
doing?'

Scores of people were standing on the roof, at the very
edge. Faces blank, they stared ahead like robots, seemingly

unaware that death waited only a single step in front of them.

'Well, no one knows,' Jackie replied. 'It just happened. Like they've been hypnotised.'

'Hypnotised!' said Jo. 'Doctor! This has to be the work of the M–'

The Doctor waved her to silence. 'Keep looking up, Jo.'

She did. Above them, almost like a roof, was a strange, rocky shape, more alien than anything she'd ever seen.

'First there was the creature on the telly. They said it was a hoax, but then they always say that, don't they? Like when the pig flew into Big Ben. Then this turned up.' Jackie folded her arms disapprovingly, unimpressed with the cheek of the alien visitors.

'It's an asteroid,' said the Doctor. 'An asteroid with engines. A masterful piece of engineering.'

'Masterf–'

'Just an expression, Jo.'

'Anyway, now you're awake again, you can sort it all out, can't you?' said Jackie.

'Awake again,' the Doctor muttered under his breath, so quietly only Jo heard him. 'Regeneration crisis, perhaps? Yes, that would make sense.' Then, louder, 'We need to find this woman, this Harriet Jones.'

'Well, there's Downing Street,' said Jackie. 'Or maybe

UNIT HQ.' The other three stared at her. 'What?' she asked.

'You know about UNIT?' said Mike.

Jackie rolled her eyes. 'What is it with you? You know I do . . .' She paused for a moment, then said in almost a shriek, 'You're *not* them, are you? You're something else, Slitheen or something. Oh my god! You're going to unzip yourselves any moment, aren't you?'

'I've certainly got no plans to unzip myself,' Mike began, but Jackie was already off and running, past graffitied walls, and up a concrete staircase, until she vanished through a door.

'Number forty-eight,' said Jo, noting which door she entered.

'Come on, we'd better follow her,' said the Doctor.

It would have been easy to get inside Flat 48 with its broken windows, but the Doctor knocked on the door instead. 'Go away!' came a shout from the other side.

The Doctor sighed and bent to the letterbox. 'I assure you that we are not Slitheen, whatever they are,' he called through it. 'And I most definitely am the Doctor.'

'Prove it! How many hearts have you got?'

'Two!'

'Well, anyone can *say* that . . .'

The front door opened slightly, a security chain holding the gap at only a few inches. A hand crept out, holding the business end of a stethoscope.

The Doctor looked extremely indignant, but Jo made 'go on!' gestures until he gave in and stood close enough for Jackie to hold the stethoscope against his chest. She placed it on one side of his ruffled shirt, then the other. The stethoscope was withdrawn.

'Satisfied?' said the Doctor impatiently.

In answer, the chain was removed and the door fully opened.

'All right. You can come in. But if I see a hint of a zip being pulled, I'm out of here.'

The three time travellers followed Jackie inside. The first thing any of them noticed was a large Christmas-tree-shaped hole in one of the internal walls.

'Don't know what the council are going to say about that,' Jackie said. 'They got out of fixing Sandra's bathroom because they said she did it herself, but I don't think the sink can have been properly fixed to the wall. I mean, it should be able to take the weight of one woman trying to fix a shower curtain, even if she was thrown out of Slimming World for using KitKat fingers to scoop up the low-fat hummus.'

Jo just nodded. It seemed easiest.

'We need to find the location of the prime minister,' said the Doctor. 'If we can find out what's going on, we may be able to help those people up there.'

'Well, go and do one of your special secret searches on the computer, Mickey,' said Jackie. 'You know where it is.'

She gestured vaguely towards a door and Mike took the cue and went through it. A few moments later he came out again. 'I can't see a computer in there,' he said.

'What?' Jackie sounded indignant. 'I don't believe it. Has someone nicked the laptop? Oh, honestly, you have to bolt things down or they walk. Let me see . . . Hang on, what are you talking about? There it is.'

Jackie was pointing at a flat silver object on the table. She went over to it and opened it up.

'That tiny box is a computer?' said Mike, stunned. 'I thought it was one of those new sandwich-toaster things. Where's the rest of it?'

'What rest of it?' Jackie dropped into a chair suddenly, as though someone had punched her in the stomach. 'You're not them, are you? You're not Mickey. That's not my Rose.'

Jo pulled out another chair and sat down. She shook her head. 'No. I'm not Rose. My name's Jo Grant. But this really is the Doctor.'

'So . . .' Jackie turned to the Doctor, her face haunted.

'So what's happened to her? What's happened to my Rose? Did you get tired of her? Trade her in for a new model? Or is she . . . Is she . . .?' Tears welled.

The Doctor huffed. 'I've never known a Rose —' he began, but Jackie didn't take that well.

'You've forgotten her already?' Jackie said, furious now. 'How *dare* you! After all she did for you! Going back to certain death to save you!'

'If she went to certain death, it stands to reason —'

Jo shot a fierce look at the Doctor, who actually got the message for once and stopped talking. Jo leaned forward and put her arm round Jackie's shoulder. 'It's not anything like that. Look, let's make everyone a nice cup of tea and I'll try to explain.'

They went out to the kitchen, and Jo continued as Jackie put the kettle on. 'You see, I don't think the Doctor's met your Rose yet.'

'What?'

'You know he can time-travel, right?'

'Yes, I know. But, every time I see my Rose, it's a bit later. I thought he'd always turn up in order, you know?' Then she looked haunted again. 'No. She told me earlier. She told me she'd been back to see her dad, that I'd even seen her then, not knowing who she was. So, if she could go back to her own past, I suppose the Doctor can come forward from his.'

Jo nodded. 'That's right.'

'So, if my Rose is with the Doctor in the future . . .'

'Yes?'

'What's happened to you? Where did you go?'

Jo's mouth dropped open as the truth of her words hit home and she stared at Jackie, horrified.

'I mean, it's bad enough knowing your daughter's dropped everything to be with some spaceman, but I thought . . . I thought she was his first. I didn't know he made a habit of it, dragging girls off into his machine. How many does he get through? Does he get tired of them and dump them on some planet somewhere? Or do they get zapped and he has to get a replacement? How many have there been between you and Rose? How many were there before you?'

'I . . . I don't know,' Jo stuttered.

Her mind raced to the TARDIS, both spaceship and sanctuary. Was it also a Bluebeard's chamber? Were the mementoes she'd stumbled across now and then – a hairslide, a red cap, a mascara wand – the last remaining traces of unnamed women who'd once accepted a ride into time and space with the Doctor? Jo shivered.

'Jo! Come here. Look at this bizarre mistletoe.'

She welcomed the interruption and almost ran out of

the kitchen. There was Mike Yates, a grin on his face and a sprig of mistletoe in his hand. 'It's got *blue* berries!' he said incredulously. He held it up for Jo to see.

'Most unusual,' the Doctor agreed, taking the sprig from Mike for a closer inspection. The smile faded from his lips. In front of Jo's eyes, his skin began to pale. His cheeks hollowed, his eyes seeming to bulge out of their sockets. The mistletoe was growing, tendrils crawling down his arms.

'Doctor!' Jo yelled as she tried to pull the leafy stems away from him.

'Stop, Jo! The more you pull, the tighter they'll hold on.'

'What can we do?' asked Mike helplessly, as the vines wrapped themselves round the Doctor's neck.

'Mistletoe's a parasite,' croaked the Doctor. 'It takes nutrients from its host – sometimes fatally. Find . . . alternative . . . food source.'

'Leave it to me!' Jackie ran out of the kitchen. She had a Christmas pudding in one hand, and she lobbed it at the Doctor. The contents of a bottle followed. 'And don't forget the brandy!'

The Doctor sighed with relief as the mistletoe fell away, sating itself on the pudding and brandy instead. His cheeks plumped up, his skin pinkened.

'That's better,' he said. 'Thank you.'

'Murderous mistletoe!' said Jo. 'That has "work of the Master" written all over it.'

'That's not what the Doctor – the other Doctor – said,' said Jackie. 'It was something to do with fish. And batteries. Things attracted by your energy? They set booby traps.'

'There's another one!' yelled Jo, quickly moving away from a snowman ornament that had started to rock violently back and forth, its carrot nose flashing orange, as a version of *The Twelve Days of Christmas* – slightly out of tune – blasted from its base.

While Jo, Mike and the Doctor backed away, Jackie went over and hit the snowman on the head. It stopped its gyrations and fell silent. 'No, it's just faulty, that's all,' she said. 'Went off in the middle of the night the other day. I nearly had a fit.'

'Never mind that now,' said the Doctor. 'My research on the computer suggests that UNIT has finally realised that having a big sign outside a building saying "UNIT Headquarters" is perhaps not the best thing for a top-secret government organisation. They now have an HQ hidden under the Tower of London.'

'Wow,' said Mike. 'I wonder what the Brig would have to say about that – sharing a home with the crown jewels. So, that's our next stop. How do we get there? Flying car?

Hoverboard? Personal transmat?'

'Number seventy-eight bus,' said Jackie.

'Hoverbus?'

'You'll be lucky if you get a double-decker.'

Mike sighed. 'So much for the future.'

'I think a short hop by TARDIS might be better,' said the Doctor. 'Come on, Jo, Mike.'

Jo and Mike followed, as instructed. To Jo's surprise, Jackie clearly intended to join them.

'Better than sitting around here, worrying about my Rose,' she said. 'I'd rather feel I was doing something.'

They ventured out into the cold. Into the TARDIS, then out of the TARDIS in moments. They were within the grounds of the tower itself. There were people standing high on the roof of the fortress, a mix of tourists and uniformed officials, all close to the edge. Still in danger. Jo's heart leaped into her mouth. A single step forward was all that separated them, like the people on top of the block of flats, from falling to their deaths.

The Doctor looked around, orienting himself, then led them towards a beefeater standing near Traitors' Gate.

'Good afternoon. I'm the Doctor,' said the Doctor.

The beefeater sighed. 'Yes, of course you are.' He made no attempt to move.

'I need to see the prime minister. Or whoever's in charge.'

'Yeah, right.'

'Yes. Right,' said the Doctor firmly, producing his UNIT pass and waving it in front of the man's nose.

The beefeater grabbed it. 'This expired thirty years ago. But I'll give you your due – it's a better effort than most.'

'What are you talking about, man? I demand you let us in this minute.'

'Look, we usually get about three "Doctors" a week. Since the prime minister's appeal on TV, we've had seven of 'em today alone. OK, I'm impressed. You've done your homework, you've found us – not that I can either confirm or deny what it is you've found – and you know about this shadowy Doctor bloke who might look like anyone. But, right now, we're in the middle of a crisis, and you're getting in the way. So just hop it, will you?'

Jo saw the fury rising in the Doctor's eyes and jumped in. 'He really *is* the Doctor, you know,' she said. 'I'm his assistant, Jo Grant. I work for UNIT too.'

'Yes, like I said, good effort. You've even got the window-dressing right. They don't always bother bringing a girl with 'em. Probably cos most wouldn't know a girl if they tripped over one.'

Now it was Jo's turn to get indignant. 'Window-dressing! Of all the chauvinistic –'

This time Mike stepped in to calm the storm. 'Now, you can see *I'm* a UNIT officer.' He indicated his khaki beret.

'Oh, come on,' the beefeater replied. 'That's not even the right colour, and the badge is totally wrong. And you stink of brandy.'

Mike stared the man in the eye. 'I am Captain Mike Yates of the United Nations Intelligence Taskforce. I am not drunk, and I demand –'

He broke off as the beefeater burst out laughing. 'You can't even get the name right! It's *Unified* Intelligence. And who are you supposed to be?' the guard continued as Jackie stepped forward. 'The UNIT tea lady?'

'Listen, you!' Jackie began, putting her hands on her hips. 'You might think you're a big shot, standing there in your little skirt and funny hat, but people's lives are in danger.'

Jo gave a gasp. 'That laugh! Yes! I know who this is! Doctor, it's the Master! That's why he won't let us in!'

'Sorry, Jo,' said the Doctor. 'I think you're confusing "architect of evil" with "sceptical jobsworth". Quite frankly, I'd rather deal with the Master.' He turned back to the man and gestured up at the roofs and ramparts. 'Those are your colleagues up there. Friends, loved ones. You might be standing in the way of their only chance. You have to let me in!'

As he spoke, the people on the roof suddenly came back to life. Heads were shaken as they leaped back or were dragged from the edge to safety.

'Oh,' said the Doctor, looking surprised. 'Well, that's good.'

There was a beeping from the beefeater's wrist and he pulled back his sleeve to reveal a small monitor screen. 'There,' he said, waving at them. 'Proof that the prime minister's not here anyway, so you might as well make yourselves scarce.'

Jackie leaped forward and grabbed his wrist. 'Rose! There's my Rose with her! Hang on, that looks like Bloxham Road! She's only round the corner from home!'

'And who's that dish with her?' gasped Jo, leaning over Jackie's shoulder.

Jackie shot her a sideways look. 'That's the Doctor.'

'Come along, Jo,' said the Doctor, as she stared at him in amazement and – it has to be said – a small amount of wistfulness.

The TARDIS landed in Jackie's sitting room.

'Doctor! Doctor!' The plaintive call was coming from elsewhere in the flat.

'I know that voice!' cried Jo.

There was another sound too, beneath the voice. *Two turtle doves, and a partridge in a pear tree. On the eleventh day of Christmas . . .*

They followed the sounds. On the floor, tied up in tinsel, was a bearded man dressed in black. Behind him sat the dancing snowman, still belting out its tuneless carol.

'The Master!' gasped Jo. 'I knew it! He was behind it all along.'

'My dear Miss Grant,' said the Master. 'I can assure you I'm not "behind" anything. Yes, I followed the Doctor here. Yes, I planned to ally myself with the Sycorax and enslave Earth. But for the last hour I have been lying here, forced to listen to what must be by now the twelve *hundred* days of Christmas!'

'The tinsel must be another booby trap!' said Mike. 'Because he's a Time Lord too, it must have activated when he got too near the Christmas tree.'

'If you would release me from my bonds, I give you my word I will leave without hurting either you or the people of this planet.'

'You can't trust him, Doctor!' cried Jo.

'I think in this case I can, Jo,' the Doctor replied. 'I have to let him go. I think –' he picked up the snowman and removed its battery – 'I think he's suffered enough.'

Released, the Master entered Jackie's kitchen. A giant pink American-style fridge vanished with a wheezing, groaning sound.

'Oh, that's a shame,' said Jackie. 'I've always wanted one of those fridges. Anyway, I'm going to love you and leave you. I need to go and find Rose.'

The Doctor held out a hand. 'I look forward to meeting you for the first time,' he said.

Jackie paused for a moment, then said, 'I can't ask him. The other you. But it's still you, so you understand him, don't you? Will he – will *you* just leave her one day? Abandon her?'

The Doctor shook his head solemnly. 'No. I can promise you that. It's not me who leaves them. Not ever.' Then he smiled. 'Anyway, if Rose is anything like her mother, I wouldn't dare!'

Jackie nodded, a quick, fierce nod of understanding. 'Thank you.'

'So, home then?' asked Mike eagerly, as Jackie hurried off and out of the flat.

'Yes, Mike, back to the TARDIS,' said the Doctor.

Jo was staring out of the broken window. 'Maybe we should stay for a bit. There's still an alien spaceship to deal with!'

The large asteroid-shaped ship began to fly away.

'Well,' said Jo, 'we need to make sure it doesn't come back.'

Much to their amazement, the ship suddenly exploded.

'We could just stay,' Jo continued regardless, 'to see if Rose is all right and say hello to this other Doctor . . .'

'Jo!' exclaimed the Doctor.

'Oh, all right! Let's go,' said Jo resignedly.

They headed back into the TARDIS. As the Doctor set the controls, Jo said, 'Is that true? That you never leave them. I mean us. I mean . . . me.'

'It's true,' said the Doctor. 'One day you'll fly the nest, Jo. But I'll never push you out of it.'

And Jo smiled. Because that knowledge was the best Christmas present she'd ever received.

THREE WISE MEN

Written by Richard Dungworth

Illustrated by Rob Biddulph

Christmas Eve, 1968
200,000 miles from Earth

Lieutenant Colonel William A. Anders could feel the press of the Command/Service Module's acceleration as its rocket engine continued to fire. He tried to stay focused on monitoring the burn.

'Two minutes,' called Colonel Frank Borman, Mission Commander, from the other end of the CSM's main control panel. 'How's it doing, Bill?'

'Great shape.' Anders' gaze flitted between the numerous dials, gauges and indicators ranged on the console in front of him. 'Pressures are holding. Helium's coming down nicely.

All other systems are go.'

The capsule's third crew couch, between those of Anders and Borman, was occupied by Captain James A. Lovell Jr, Command Module Pilot. Lovell was as cool as they came, but even he was visibly on edge. His eyes were glued to the navigation-system read-outs. The atmosphere on board had not been this tense since the long minutes before launch.

The launch. Anders would not forget *that* in a hurry. It was almost three days now since he and his Apollo 8 crew-mates had become the first astronauts to endure the rumbling, roaring din and crushing acceleration of a lift-off powered by NASA's mightiest-ever launch vehicle: the towering 110-metre, multi-stage *Saturn V* rocket. The five colossal F-1 engines of the *Saturn*'s first stage – each burning 2,500 litres of liquid oxygen and kerosene rocket-fuel every second – had blasted them on their way from Launch Pad 39A of the Kennedy Space Center with a combined thrust of over 34,000 kilonewtons. A hundred jumbo-jet engines could not have matched this awesome force. Perched atop the giant rocket in the Apollo CSM, Anders, Borman and Lovell had been accelerated to a staggering, record-breaking velocity of over 24,000 miles per hour.

The acceleration they were feeling right now was nothing by comparison. The CSM's single-rocket Service

Propulsion System, or SPS, generated some 91 kilonewtons of thrust – only a tiny fraction of the *Saturn V*'s power. What was strangely unnerving was that out here in space, where there was no atmosphere to conduct sound, it did so in eerie silence.

There was more than mechanics, however, behind the crew's tension. They all knew what was at stake: their lives depended on the SPS performing as planned. Apollo 8's objective was to become the first manned craft to orbit the moon. For the crew to succeed in their bold mission and make it back home safely, they needed this burn to go without a hitch.

'We're past two minutes,' reported Anders. 'Everything's looking good.'

Since leaving Earth's orbit, they had already relied on the SPS to make corrections to their course. It was thanks to two previous burns that the Apollo module, after coasting across empty space for sixty-six hours, was now perfectly positioned to attempt Lunar Orbital Insertion.

The insertion manoeuvre required the longest burn yet. The engine's thrust was needed to slow the drifting module down, so that the moon's gravitational pull would capture it in a stable orbit. In preparation, Jim Lovell had used the CSM's small Reaction Control System jets to angle it at the exact reverse pitch specified in the mission flight plan.

There was no room for error. The precise direction and timing of the burn were crucial. If it reduced the CSM's velocity too much, or steered it too low, the moon's gravity would drag the little craft into a slow dive. It would crash into the bleak lunar landscape.

NASA's technicians had calculated a burn time of four minutes and two seconds.

Lovell let out a long, controlled breath. 'Longest four minutes *I* ever spent,' he said, smiling grimly.

Anders checked the propellant pressures again and gave his commander another update.

'Three minutes. We're looking good, Frank.' *So long as the guys back home did the math right,* he thought. *Else it won't be much of a Christmas.*

They were now entering the final stage of the burn. Lovell began marking the time remaining until the scheduled shutdown.

'Forty-eight seconds.'

As if the insertion manoeuvre wasn't already nerve-racking enough, they were having to perform it while out of touch with Mission Control. Just under a quarter of an hour ago, the CSM's drift had carried it round the moon's far side, causing a temporary loss of radio contact with Earth. Loss

of signal had occurred at 068:58:45 Ground Elapsed Time –
sixty-eight hours, fifty-eight minutes and forty-five seconds
after launch – exactly as predicted.

Lovell's final words to Houston before the cut-off echoed
in Anders' mind. *We'll see you on the other side.* Anders crossed
his fingers – even an astronaut could be superstitious – and
hoped his friend was right.

'Twenty-eight,' declared Lovell. 'Stand by.'

Borman was poised to carry out a manual override, in
case the SPS's automatic control system let them down.

'Five . . . four . . .'

Anders took over from Lovell for the final seconds.
'Three . . . two . . . one.'

'Shutdown.' On Borman's mark, Anders felt the pressure
against his acceleration couch ease. The engine had died.

'Verify thrust is off. Helium valves are OK. Pressure is
static.'

Quickly and efficiently, the three astronauts began the
well-rehearsed sequence of post-burn system checks.

'Flight Recorder OK.'

'SPS, Gimbal Motors, four, off, slowly.'

'OK.'

'One, off.'

'Got it.'

'Two, off.'

'Got it . . .'

It was only when the last of many switches had been
thrown, and the CSM's new status verified, that they allowed
themselves to relax.

Anders felt a flood of relief. 'Congratulations,
gentlemen!' He beamed. 'We're at zero-zero!'

The crucial manoeuvre had gone like clockwork. The
team back in Houston's calculations had been spot on. The
CSM had now entered a stable orbit round the moon –
something no manned spacecraft had ever done before.

Anders read the Mission Timer display: 069:14:32.
Mission Control would have to wait a little while to hear the
good news; it would be another twenty minutes before the
Apollo module emerged from the moon's shadow and its
communication antenna could reconnect them with Houston.

For the module's crew, however, the wait was over.

They were now just over three hundred metres from
the moon, and the view was breathtaking. Through the
small rendezvous window in his side of the module, Anders
marvelled at the strange, alien world. It might have been
crafted from plaster of Paris. Its barren, dusty terrain was a
pale brownish-grey. It was pock-marked with vast craters –
the scars of ancient meteorite strikes. Anders felt the thrill of

'Oh, very well,' said the Doctor with a sniff. 'Investigate if you must. But don't lose sight of the idea that this may be a trap!'

All I Want For Christmas

Written by Jacqueline Rayner

Illustrated by Nick Harris

'We're being chased,' Zoe told the audience. 'Has anyone seen a great big orange alien?'
'It's behind you!' shouted someone in the crowd, thinking this was part of the show.

A Comedy of Terrors
Written by Colin Brake
Illustrated by Melissa Castrillón

*The smile faded from his lips. In front of Jo's eyes, his skin
began to pale . . . The mistletoe was growing,
tendrils crawling down his arms.*

The Christmas Inversion

Written by Jacqueline Rayner

Illustrated by Sara Gianassi

*'As charming as your delightfully quaint vessel is, I think it might
be best for you to come aboard mine.'*

Three Wise Men

Written by Richard Dungworth

Illustrated by Rob Biddulph

the explorer gazing on an unknown land.

'You want to take some pictures, Bill?' The ever-efficient Borman was already checking the flight plan for their next task. 'We're all done with the SPS. Camera prep's up next.'

Anders had been designated chief photographer. It was his responsibility to take pictures of the lunar surface. NASA hoped to use these images to map the moon in as much detail as possible, so as to choose potential landing sites for a future mission.

What would that *be like?* wondered Anders as he continued to gaze out at the desolate lunar landscape. *To actually land down there.* It was just one vast nothingness. No life, no sound, no colour. He felt a sudden, overwhelming swell of loneliness. He thought of his family, so very, very far away, enjoying the Christmas festivities . . .

'Bill?'

Borman's voice brought Anders back to the here and now.

'Camera prep,' he confirmed. 'Got it.'

He pushed himself out of his couch and over towards the module's lower bay, where the photographic kit was stowed. He was getting the hang of moving around in free fall, and the space sickness he and the others had suffered in the first days of the mission had more or less worn off.

The CSM carried a range of photographic equipment, including enough magazines of film to capture nearly a thousand shots. Anders helped himself to a Hasselblad 70mm camera from one of the storage lockers. He opened another to find a suitable lens – and noticed something odd.

Every single piece of equipment on board the CSM was itemised in the official Mission Stowage List. The crew had all studied this document so that they were familiar with exactly what kit they had at their disposal and where to find it. In light of his duties, Anders had paid particular attention to what was stowed in the photographic equipment lockers.

The brown-paper parcel crammed in on top of the camera lenses had not, Anders was certain, been on the list.

He lifted the mystery package out to take a closer look. It was the size and shape of a half-kilo bag of sugar, and was marked with an unfamiliar emblem – not NASA's standard 'meatball' insignia, but a grid-lined globe, stamped in black ink, with the initials UNIT arching round it.

Anders was puzzled. Had the guys back home packed them a Christmas surprise? He was considering opening the package, to satisfy his curiosity, when a startled cry made him turn round.

'*Holy cow!*'

Jim Lovell was gaping up at the CSM's main crew hatch,

directly above his central couch. The hatch had a small round window in it. At first Anders thought Lovell was simply awestruck by the lunar view. But, as he followed his crew-mate's wide-eyed stare, his blood froze.

There was a face outside the window.

Anders' brain locked up, flatly refusing to process the inconceivable. Like Lovell, he simply stared, stupefied.

The face was dominated by goggling eyes and an impressive set of teeth bared in a manic grin. It was framed by a wild mass of curly dark hair.

Anders' mind came back to him, flooding with questions. How could anyone be out there? Where had he come from? How was he breathing without a helmet? And – again – *how* could anyone be out there?

Borman, too, was staring in disbelief.

Lovell made the first attempt to explain the inexplicable. 'Russian?' he suggested feebly.

Anders numbly shook his head. 'Can't be.'

The race between the USA and the Soviet Union to be first to the moon was very much on. But, unless American intelligence was badly mistaken, NASA were at least a nose ahead of their rivals. The Russians *couldn't* have put a cosmonaut in lunar orbit already.

But then *who*?

The face at the window took on a look of concentration. A high-pitched electronic hum was faintly, briefly audible through the triple-glazed pane. As it cut out, a mechanical rattle came from the innards of the hatch.

Borman's wide eyes darted to the ratchet handle that operated the hatch's locking mechanism. It was turning, fast, of its own accord.

'No!' Borman made a desperate lunge for the handle – but too late. With a chorus of clunks, the hatch's fifteen synchronised latches released. It swung open.

The next few moments should have been catastrophic. The air in the pressurised module should have rushed violently out through the opened hatch, into the vacuum of space beyond, carrying all three astronauts with it to an unpleasant and untimely death.

What happened instead was that the tasseled ends of an unfeasibly long, stripy scarf flopped down into the capsule to dangle close to Lovell's paled, upturned face. He shrank back as if the tassels might bite.

The owner of the multicoloured scarf then peered down through the open hatchway. He was beaming toothily at the Apollo crew.

'Greetings, my bold yuletide travellers!' he boomed in a voice like thunder. 'And compliments of the season!' He cast his gaze around the cramped interior of the Apollo capsule. 'As charming as your delightfully quaint vessel is, I think it might be best for *you* to come aboard *mine*.' He flashed another outsize grin. 'Rather roomier.' His eyes fixed on Anders' right hand, and he gave a roar of apparent delight. 'Ah-*haaa*! And do bring that along, won't you? There's a good fellow.'

Then the dangling scarf rose, and he was gone.

In the silence that followed, Anders looked first at the forgotten parcel in his hand, then to each of his dumbstruck crew-mates. Both Borman and Lovell looked as lost as he felt. NASA had trained them for every foreseeable eventuality, however improbable – but not for the impossible.

Suddenly the stranger was back.

'Come along! Chop-chop!' he roared down at them. 'An air corridor between moving craft can be tricky, you know. Not sure how long the old girl can hold it.'

And he was gone again.

Borman continued to stare wordlessly at the open hatchway. Anders could guess what was going through his mind. *What now?* What was the correct command decision when a stranger came calling in deep space? If you were invited to board his craft – to leave your own, without so much as a pressure suit – how should you proceed?

We have to go, thought Anders, curiosity overruling caution. It was their duty, surely, to find out what in the world was going on.

Borman had evidently come to the same conclusion. He reached for the rim of the crew hatch and began to pull himself through.

Lovell set off after his commander, shaking his head. 'No sleep for three days,' he muttered. 'Guess I'm having some sort of fantasy.'

Anders felt his pulse quicken as he brought up the rear. *Is that what this is?* he thought. *A fantasy?* It was certainly crazy enough.

Outside, it only got crazier.

Floating a few metres from the Apollo module, matching its drift, was a large blue wardrobe-like box. From his visits to London, Anders recognised it as a commonplace police box. The stranger stood in its open doorway, a wide-brimmed brown hat perched atop his wild curls. He was beckoning impatiently.

Borman and Lovell were already gliding across the void between the two craft. They were riding a broad current of air that Anders could feel tugging at him as he slid out of the hatchway.

Air? Here?

Anders pushed off from the hatch's rim and glided after his crew-mates. Up ahead, he saw the stranger help first Borman, then Lovell through the box's doorway. Moments later, he was being hauled across the worn wooden threshold himself, into the safety of . . . what, exactly?

The police box's interior made no sense. It was impossibly big – a large polygonal chamber lit by rows of luminous discs set in stark white-grey walls. Passages leading off it suggested the vessel's full extent was greater still. Its internal scale was mind-bending.

For all that, it was less 'roomy' than it might have been, due to the fact that the entire space was crammed with Christmas presents. Brightly gift-wrapped parcels were piled everywhere Anders looked. There were thousands upon thousands of them, in all shapes and sizes.

'Ah. Yes.' The stranger had noticed his guests' roaming eyes. 'Sorry about the clutter. That's the drawback of a dimensionally transcendental space. Devilish to keep tidy.' He waded through the sea of presents to an out-of-place antique hatstand, on which he hung his battered brown hat. 'Thankfully, this little lot all has to be offloaded by the morrow. I've taken on a bet, you see. With an old acquaintance.'

He made his way across to a control console that

sprouted from the centre of the chamber like a large, hi-tech hexagonal mushroom.

'Bit of a self-satisfied old soul, between you and me. Fame's rather gone to his head. Seems to think he's the only one capable of a little super-luminary pan-terrestrial distribution.' He grinned another huge grin. 'Thought I'd show him otherwise.'

Looking suddenly more serious, he brought a hand down on the console top. 'Only trouble is, the old girl's let me down. Gone on the blink. Just when time – or *defying* it – is of the essence. Which is why –' he beamed at the bewildered astronauts – 'I have enlisted the help of *you* fine gentlemen!'

The three men stared back at him uncomprehendingly.

'Who *are* you?' said Borman weakly. 'Where did you come from?'

'I'm the Doctor!' boomed the stranger, as if it went without saying. 'From Gallifrey. Currently of no fixed abode.' He approached Borman with a look of purpose. 'Now, I believe you come bearing gifts, mmm?' He held out a hand, palm upturned.

Borman looked blank.

'Your *pocket*, man!' growled the Doctor with sudden impatience. He gestured to the pocket in the shoulder of Borman's in-flight overalls.

'But . . . I don't . . .' faltered Borman. 'There's nothing in –' As his fingers delved into the pocket, he broke off. Looking ever more mystified, he took out a slim package wrapped in brown paper. Numbly, he placed it in the Doctor's outstretched hand. Anders saw that it bore the same black emblem as his own mystery package.

'Thank you, commander,' rumbled the Doctor. He tore open the packet. Inside was a flat disc of jet-black material the size of a jam-jar lid. Its surface was veined with fine silver lines. The Doctor examined it approvingly.

'Excellent!'

He turned his attention to his second guest.

'And now the famous Mister Lovell, hero of Apollo 13! Quite the adventure, eh? Real skin-of-your-teeth stuff. Prime example of your stubborn species at their excellent best!'

'Erm . . . thank you?' mumbled Lovell, looking utterly nonplussed.

Your species? thought Anders. *Apollo 13?*

The Doctor held out his palm again.

Lovell knew the routine now. Searching his shoulder pocket, he discovered a second slim, logo-stamped packet. He handed it over.

It yielded an equally mysterious object that looked rather like a tiny glass tuning-fork with red-tipped prongs.

'Splendid!' roared the Doctor. 'And now –' he looked to Anders – 'last, but by no means least.'

Anders took his turn to surrender his mystery 'gift'. The Doctor took the parcel, opened the top of its wrapping and peered eagerly inside.

'Ah-*haaaa*!'

With finger and thumb, he plucked out something small and orange – and popped it straight into his mouth. As he began to chew, a blissful expression came over his face. Swallowing, he offered the open package to his guests.

'Jelly Baby, anyone?'

The three astronauts only gawped.

'No? Suit yourselves.'

The Doctor took another sweet, then dropped the package into one pocket of his long brown coat. He moved back across to the central console.

'I was a little concerned my message might not reach the Brigadier,' he said, carefully placing the black disc on the console's surface. 'It's about time those bumblers at UNIT made themselves useful.'

He produced a metallic, torch-like tool from his coat. As he touched its tip to the black disc, the tool began to emit the same high-pitched hum Anders had heard through the hatch window.

'They've secretly built up quite a collection of non-terrestrial technology over the last hundred years,' continued the Doctor over the humming. 'Not that they have a clue, mind you, what most of it does.' He drew back the tool, extracting a long, thin silvery strand from the disc. 'Stuck in Earth space with a dicky Dematerialisation Circuit, they were the obvious source for the components I needed.' He quickly wound the glittering strand round the prongs of the tuning-fork gizmo. 'The tricky bit was how to get them here.' He looked up to treat his guests to another wild-eyed smile. 'Lucky you were in the neighbourhood, eh?'

Without warning, he gave the side of the console a firm thump. A hinged panel in its underside swung down.

The Doctor grasped the strange modified component between his fingertips. He crouched down and ducked his head below the jutting console. 'I can't splice this new looper in while she's running hot,' he continued as he worked beneath it. There was more of the high-pitched humming. 'I'll have to power down the tertiary cells. She'll not sustain that corridor without them.'

More humming. Then silence.

The Doctor's face reappeared, frowning.

'Still here?' he asked brusquely. 'That was your cue to leave. Don't you have a historic mission to get back to?'

He returned to his task.

Anders, Borman and Lovell exchanged looks. As they turned to leave the way they had come, the booming voice called after them.

'I'll see if she can nudge you back on track once she's in the pink. We mustn't spoil NASA's precious flight plans now, must we?'

Once outside, it took less than a minute for all three astronauts to make the return trip along the air corridor and through the CSM's open hatchway. They hurriedly worked together to close and reseal the hatch. At last, it was secure.

A long silence followed. Three minds struggled to get to grips with what had just happened.

Borman was the first to speak. 'How long till acquisition, Bill?'

Anders steered himself across to the main control panel. The Mission Timer read 069:31:10. The predicted Ground Elapsed Time for re-establishing contact with Mission Control was 069:36:00.

'Just under five minutes.'

'Five minutes. OK.' Borman looked thoughtful. 'And once we *can* talk to Houston again –' he smiled wryly at his two crew-mates – 'what exactly, gentlemen, do we tell them?'

Anders knew what Borman was driving at. If they were

to describe their bizarre encounter to their colleagues back on
Earth, there could be only one likely response: total disbelief.
NASA's team of highly rational engineers and scientists could
hardly be expected to swallow the news that the latest phase
of their multi-billion-dollar Apollo programme had just
served, without their knowledge, to courier some bits and
bobs of alien technology, plus a handsome supply of Jelly
Babies, from an underground intelligence organisation to a
stranger from somewhere called Gallifrey.

A guy in a technicolour scarf, Anders imagined reporting to
Houston. *With his own space-going police box. He was trying to win a
bet with Santa.*

Mission Control would conclude – quite reasonably
– that the extreme stress and isolation of the crew's heroic
space voyage had resulted in total nervous collapse; that they
had, in short, lost their minds. They would be judged unfit
for further involvement in the programme. On their return to
Earth, their careers as astronauts would be over.

Unless . . . thought Anders, in a flash of inspiration.

'The DSE,' he muttered. Then, excitedly, to the others,
'We've got the DSE!'

The Data Storage Equipment was a sophisticated
recording machine wired up to the module's key systems.
Its role was to make a live recording of essential flight

information on a ribbon of fourteen-track magnetic tape. It was capable of storing up to two hours of flight data – including any on-board conversation. At regular intervals, Mission Control 'dumped' the tape's contents back to Earth via the radio link. This gave Houston the opportunity to check vital system readings and advise the crew accordingly. After each data dump, the DSE began a fresh recording.

Anders had reset the recorder shortly before loss of signal. It was now going about its business, its large twin reels turning steadily. A good portion of the tape was already wound round the right-hand reel. It would hold data from the last half hour. This was what Anders was counting on.

'There'll be audio of the Doctor!' he explained. 'And maybe a safety-fail alert, too, from when the hatch opened.'

Borman came to join him, understanding dawning in his eyes. The DSE's recording ought to offer *some* proof, at least, of the Doctor's improbable presence. It would support their unbelievable tale.

As he and Borman watched the DSE's turning reels, Anders suddenly experienced a momentary sense of disorientation. For a split second, his vision blurred. He had a fleeting loss of balance.

Then everything was normal again.

Normal, but not the same.

Anders stared at the DSE. It was running smoothly, just as it had been a moment ago. Now, however, its left-hand reel was almost full. There was barely any tape – fifteen minutes' worth at most – on the right-hand reel.

From the look on Borman's face, Anders knew he had felt the jolt too.

'What just happened, Frank?'

Borman didn't answer. He reached for the switch that activated the DSE's on-board voice recorder, and flicked it off. He looked at Anders gravely.

'Remember the last thing he said? About putting us "back on track"?'

Grasping Borman's implication, Anders frowned. 'How could he –'

'Guys!' Lovell's shout was urgent. He was poring over the main control panel. 'You need to see this.'

As Anders and Borman joined him, Lovell gestured to the Mission Timer. Anders read its display.

069:14:32.

The same reading as immediately after the insertion burn.

'But that's *impossible!*'

'Uh-huh,' agreed Lovell. 'Same way as a bigger-on-the-inside space cupboard is. The navigation readings tally, too. See for yourselves.'

There was no denying it. They were right back where they had been – or *when* they had been – before the Doctor's surprise appearance. Any chance of using the DSE's recording to support their tall story was gone. And the story had just got a whole lot taller.

Lovell was looking up at the hatch above him. Anders followed his gaze. There was no trace of the blue box.

'So,' said Borman grimly. 'We've got nothing. Just our own testimony.' He was silent for a few seconds, then seemed to reach a decision.

'Gentlemen, it seems to me that it's in everyone's best interests if we keep this to ourselves. The eyes of the world are upon us. Can you imagine the harm it would do – to the programme, to NASA, perhaps even to the future of international space exploration – if we were to appear to have lost our grip on reality? I propose we put this . . . *episode* behind us. Go on with the flight plan, and say nothing to the folks back home.'

Anders couldn't help feeling that Borman was right.

'It *would* be a shame to spoil everyone's Christmas,' said Lovell.

Borman looked from one crew-mate to the other. 'Are we agreed, then?'

Anders nodded.

'Agreed,' said Lovell.

Borman looked relieved. 'Good.' He gave his crew-mates another wry smile. 'Then let's get back to making history.' He flicked the DSE's voice-recorder switch back on. 'You want to take some pictures, Bill?'

And, with that, the three Apollo astronauts resumed their mission duties, doing their best to focus their thoughts on the historic enterprise in which they were engaged – and not on their encounter with the remarkable stranger from Gallifrey.

It seemed like the wise thing to do.

SONTAR'S LITTLE
HELPERS

Written by Mike Tucker

Illustrated by Staffan Gnosspelius

Tegan pulled open the door to her room and stuck her head out into the TARDIS corridor. During her time with the Doctor she had got used to the various noises that the time machine made. She couldn't exactly say that the sounds it made were familiar, but she *was* acutely aware when a noise wasn't one she'd heard before. And she didn't recognise this noise at all.

'So you heard it too?'

A voice from further down the corridor made her jump.

'Turlough!' Tegan turned and glared at him. 'Do you have to sneak up on people like that?'

'Sorry.' Turlough looked hurt. 'I heard something so I came out to investigate.'

'Yeah, well, me too.' Tegan pulled the door to her room closed and set off along the corridor, Turlough hurrying to catch up with her.

'It's coming from the console room,' he said.

'Yes.' Tegan frowned. 'And it sounds a bit like . . . singing!'

The two of them reached the door to the control room and paused, listening to the tuneless sounds coming from beyond.

'It's the Doctor,' said Turlough in astonishment.

Tegan pushed open the door and the two of them peered through. The Doctor was standing with his back to them, his attention firmly on the controls of the recently refurbished central console. He was singing loudly to himself, arms waving as if conducting some invisible orchestra. As tuneless as it was, Tegan laughed as she realised the Doctor was singing a Christmas carol.

'Many happy returns of the season, Doctor!'

He jumped at the sound of her voice, spinning round and giving her an embarrassed smile. 'Ah! Tegan. Turlough. Good morning.'

'What on earth are you doing?' Turlough said, grinning broadly.

The Doctor bustled around the console sheepishly.

'Well, now that the TARDIS has been fully refurbished and is totally reliable, I thought I'd materialise to get a bearing to synchronise the temporal balance cones, and I discovered that the date here is December twenty-fourth.'

'Christmas Eve?' Tegan's face lit up.

'Yes, relatively speaking. Perhaps not on your personal timeline, but as far as this portion of space–time is concerned.'

Turlough grimaced. 'Christmas. They always made such a fuss about it at Brendon. I never enjoyed it myself.'

'Aw, Turlough. Don't be such a spoilsport,' said Tegan. 'I love Christmas!'

A sudden harsh beeping cut across the gentle hum of the room, and a small red light started to flash on one of the panels.

'What was that about the new console being totally reliable, Doctor?' Tegan asked.

Turlough hurried over to look at the read-out. 'It's not an internal fault. It's a signal.'

'It's a Mayday!' The Doctor darted round the console, his fingers dancing over the multitude of buttons and switches. 'It's a long way off, but if I can just lock on to the beacon . . .'

With a grind of ancient engines, the central column

of the TARDIS started to rise and fall as the Doctor sent it spinning into the vortex. From past experience, Tegan knew to hang on tightly to the edge of the console – but the flight was short and, by the Doctor's standards, relatively smooth.

As soon as the time rotor stopped moving, the Doctor bounded over to the scanner control, opening the two huge shutters that concealed the TARDIS's view screen. Tegan and Turlough hurried to join him, and looked out at a tiny spacecraft hanging before them in the inky blackness of space. Below it was a vast, pale planet, the surface gleaming brightly as if covered in frost. A planet of ice – quite the fitting place to visit at Christmas.

'Is that the spacecraft sending the Mayday?' asked Tegan.

'Yes.' The Doctor peered at the screen intently.

'It's a bit weedy.'

'It's a fighter craft!' said Turlough.

'Oh, great!' Tegan rolled her eyes. 'Have you landed us in the middle of a war?'

'No.' The Doctor sounded bemused. 'There's no conflict that I'm aware of in this part of the galaxy. Not for centuries yet, at least.'

'Er, Doctor.' Turlough pointed at the screen. 'It seems we're not the only ones to have answered the Mayday.'

A huge, bulky freighter was slowly sliding into view, plasma venting from its engines as it came to a halt next to the fighter craft.

The Doctor leaped into action, readjusting the controls and bringing the console to life again.

'Where are we going now?' asked Tegan.

'To say hello to our fellow visitors!'

The cool, dark calm of the freighter's cargo bay was shattered by the grinding, rasping noise of the TARDIS materialising.

The freighter's complex recognition software immediately scanned the new arrival and, identifying the lettering on the TARDIS as human in origin, sent a series of commands to environmental control. There was a soft hiss as atmosphere was transferred to the hold. Dozens of LED lights flickered into life, bathing everything in a soft, bluish glow.

With a rattle of the lock, the TARDIS door swung open and the Doctor stepped out into the cargo bay, sniffing the air distastefully.

'Is it safe?' Tegan's voice came from behind him.

'Yes. A bit musty, but quite breathable.' Putting on his hat, the Doctor wandered across to a huge bank of cargo containers.

Tegan stepped out of the TARDIS and looked around

cautiously. Turlough followed her, pulling the door closed behind him. The Doctor was examining one of the hundreds of cargo containers that lined the hold, and Tegan moved to join him.

'What have you found?' she asked.

'Oh, nothing much. Just the destination of this freighter.'

Turlough peered at the signage stamped on to the boxes. 'Supplies for the colony on Loen.' He frowned. 'Loen? I've not heard of that.'

'I'm not surprised,' said the Doctor. 'Loen is a very long way out indeed. Right at the tip of one of the spiral arms of the Milky Way. It's about as far as human colonists have managed to get.'

'So this freighter is carrying supplies for the colonists?' Tegan peered at the rows of boxes. 'That's a lot of supplies.'

'Yes. Now, I wonder where –'

Before the Doctor could finish, a door at the far end of the cargo bay slid open with a hiss of hydraulics. A tall, slim robot was gliding through it towards them, mechanical arms flapping agitatedly.

'PLEASE STAND BACK! UNAUTHORISED PERSONNEL ARE NOT ALLOWED TO INTERFERE WITH THE CARGO.'

The Doctor held up his hands apologetically. 'Sorry!'

Tegan was less contrite, stepping towards the robot with her hands on her hips. 'We weren't interfering. We were just looking.'

The robot came to halt, camera eyes scanning the three time travellers.

'THIS IS A RESTRICTED AREA. I SHALL HAVE TO FILE A REPORT.' Lights began to flash in a frantic pattern across the robot's chest.

'Excuse me.' The Doctor grasped Tegan by the shoulders and gently pulled her to one side. 'May I ask who we are addressing?'

The chasing lights slowed. 'I AM P011Y S.C.A. OF THE LONG-RANGE FREIGHTER *ST NICHOLAS*.'

'S.C.A.' The Doctor frowned. 'Society for Creative Anachronism?'

The robot gave the electronic equivalent of a sigh of frustration. 'SENIOR COMMAND AUTOMATON.'

'Command?' asked Tegan. 'You're in charge here?'

'I MOST CERTAINLY AM.' The robot almost sounded offended. 'NOW, IF YOU WILL PLEASE STAND ASIDE, I MUST MAKE A FULL INVENTORY OF THE CARGO.'

The robot gave a series of electronic bleeps and clicks. Immediately hundreds of smaller robots emerged from a multitude of hatches in the hangar walls and started swarming all over the cargo containers.

Tegan stared in amazement. 'Are there no people on board this ship?'

'This is an unmanned freighter,' the Doctor explained. 'Probably sent to Loen centuries before the settlers themselves, allowing them to travel with minimal weight. They were a fascinating breed, those early stellar pioneers, I recall that much –'

'Doctor.' Turlough's voice cut across him. 'The history lesson is *very* interesting, but there's a reason we came here, remember? The Mayday signal?' Turlough was looking out of a huge observation window that ran the length of the cargo bay at the fighter craft, which was still floating serenely alongside them.

'You're quite right, Turlough,' the Doctor said, turning swiftly back to P011Y. 'We came here to answer a Mayday call. I'm assuming that's the reason you're here too?'

'A FALSE ALARM,' snapped the robot. 'AN UNNECESSARY DIVERSION FROM OUR SCHEDULED ROUTE.'

'Really?' The Doctor looked puzzled. 'You detected no survivors?'

'THE FIGHTER CRAFT IS UNMANNED. ITS DISTRESS BEACON WAS ON AUTOMATIC. THESE

QUESTIONS ARE WASTING TIME. WE NEED TO
GET THIS SHIP BACK ON SCHEDULE.'

'But, if there was no one on board the ship, then who –'

'Doctor!' Turlough looked alarmed. He was pointing out
of the observation window. 'There's another ship here – it's
uncloaking!'

The Doctor and Tegan hurried over just in time to see a
huge spherical spacecraft shimmer into view.

'Oh no.' The Doctor's face fell. 'A Sontaran ship. Back
into the TARDIS, quickly!'

But, before they could move, there was a harsh crackling
sound, and blue lightning lanced around the cargo bay.

A squat figure clad in jet-black armour and wearing a
gleaming domed helmet materialised in front of them. The
figure was flanked by a squad of angular metallic robots, each
of which appeared poised to attack at any moment.

The squat figure raised a stubby three-fingered claw to
point a slim tube at the Doctor's head. The Doctor slowly
raised his hands.

'You will not move.' The rasping voice echoed around
the cargo bay. 'This ship is now under my control.'

'And you are?' asked the Doctor.

'Lieutenant Braast of the Sontaran gunship *Apocalypse*.'

'THIS IS OUTRAGEOUS.' P011Y glided towards the

Sontaran, arms aloft. 'YOU ARE COMMITTING AN ACT OF PIRACY.'

'Piracy?' snarled Braast. 'How insulting! This is an act of war!'

He swung the slim tube towards the robot. There was a bright flare, a sharp crackle of energy, and P011Y's head exploded in a shower of brilliant sparks. The robot stood upright for a moment, arms still waving about, then crashed to the floor with a deafening clang. Immediately all the other robots working in the cargo bay ground to a halt, lights fading from their casings.

The Doctor took a step towards the Sontaran, his face clouded with anger. 'That was not necessary!'

Braast swung his blaster back towards the Doctor, hissing at his guard robots. 'Restrain these humanoids.'

The angular robots flanking the Sontaran surged forward, their metallic mouths chittering frantically, and wrapped metal arms and octopus legs round the Doctor and his companions.

Once his captives were secure, Braast thrust his blaster back into his belt and reached up to remove his helmet. Tegan gasped as his potato-like features were revealed.

'Sontarans are not exactly the most photogenic of species,' quipped the Doctor.

Braast tucked his helmet under his arm and leaned closer, scrutinising the Doctor carefully. 'You know my species?'

The Doctor glared at him. 'We've crossed paths once or twice.'

Braast snatched a triangular instrument from his belt and thrust it into the Doctor's face.

'Ah.' The Sontaran examined the read-out. 'A Time Lord. I might have guessed – the smug superiority should have given you away.' His lip curled in contempt. 'Pacifist degenerate.'

Braast now shifted his device to Tegan. His wide mouth twisted into a snarl of disappointment as the scanner results were displayed.

'A Terran female. *Pah!* Worthless.'

'Worthless?' Tegan was furious. 'Now just one minute!'

'Tegan.' The Doctor's voice had gone up an octave. 'This really *isn't* the time to start an argument.'

Braast ignored them; he was now staring at Turlough through narrowed eyes. 'Now *this* is a specimen with some promise.' He examined the read-out on his scanner with growing excitement. 'Yes. More than adequate!'

At an unspoken command from Braast, the robot restraining Turlough released its grip, its legs withdrawing into its casing.

'You will come with me,' snapped the Sontaran.

'Where are you taking him?' Tegan shouted.

'Braast!' The Doctor's voice had hardened. 'I'm warning you, if you harm that boy –'

Without even a glance in their direction, Braast snatched the blaster from his belt and fired. The Doctor and Tegan were enveloped in a ball of spitting, fizzing scarlet energy.

Turlough stared in horror at the contorted, agonised faces of his friends. 'Stop it! You're hurting them!'

Braast's eyes didn't leave Turlough's face. 'What is your name and rank?'

'Please!' Turlough took a step towards his companions, but two of the Sontaran's robots blocked his way, chittering menacingly.

'What is your name and rank?' repeated Braast.

'My name is Vislor Turlough! I'm a Junior Ensign Commander in the Trion Navy.'

'Excellent.' Braast lowered his blaster and the awful ball of red energy faded away.

Turlough pushed past the robots and hurried over to the Doctor and Tegan. The Doctor was on his knees, gasping for breath, and Turlough led a trembling Tegan to sit down on one of the cargo crates.

'Let that be a warning to you,' hissed Braast.

'Disobedience of any kind will result in more suffering for your friends.'

'Are you all right?' Turlough was crouched in front of Tegan, concerned by how pale she had become.

'I feel like every nerve in my body has been scraped.'

'A neural lash,' the Doctor said, getting to his feet and wincing as he rubbed the back of his neck. 'Typically nasty Sontaran weapon.'

'And if you don't move, Trion, I'll do it again,' snarled Braast. Tegan tensed as the Sontaran's hand dropped to the hilt of his blaster once more.

'All right,' Turlough said, standing. 'All right! What is it that you want me to do?'

Braast grabbed hold of Turlough's arm with a stubby claw and dragged him towards the window. 'Are you capable of flying that?' He pointed at the fighter craft floating outside in the blackness.

'Yes, I should think so.' Turlough was puzzled. 'But why –'

'Then you and I shall do battle!' the Sontaran interrupted with a booming cry. 'To the death!'

Tegan watched with terror as Braast forced Turlough to clamber into a bulky pressure suit, then marched him to the airlock.

'What's going on, Doctor?' she whispered. 'Why is the Sontaran doing this?'

The Doctor sighed. 'Braast is a juvenile, probably only a few hours old.'

'Hours?' Tegan gaped at him.

'Yes. The Sontarans are a clone species,' explained the Doctor. 'It's how they maintain numbers despite ever-mounting casualties in their perpetual war with the Rutan Empire.'

'OK, so they like fighting. I get that. But where does Turlough fit into this?'

'My guess is that Braast is undergoing some sort of ritual initiation – a rite of passage, to prove his worth as a warrior. He's assessed the three of us and decided that Turlough is the best candidate to give him a good battle –' he paused – 'and presumably an honourable victory.'

Tegan was appalled. 'That's barbaric!'

'It's very similar to initiation rites found in dozens of early cultures on your own planet.'

'There's a big difference between that and this.' She stared out of the window, watching Turlough spacewalk towards the sleek fighter craft, one of the Sontaran robots alongside him. 'Is Turlough really going to be able to fly that thing, Doctor?'

'Oh, I find it best never to underestimate what Turlough is capable of,' said the Doctor. He frowned, deep in thought. 'My guess is that Braast killed the original pilot of that ship, then used the distress beacon to lure in another opponent.'

'You are quite right, Time Lord.'

The Doctor and Tegan turned from the window to find Braast standing behind them.

'The pilot was a coward, a deserter from a Skonnon battle fleet. He turned his ship and fled rather than face me in single combat.'

'So you did kill him.'

'Unfortunately, I was denied that pleasure. By the time I had tracked him down again he had merely run out of air.' The Sontaran grimaced. 'There is no honour in suffocation.'

'That's awful.' Tegan didn't try to hide her revulsion.

'It is of no consequence. His actions indicate that he would not have been a worthy opponent. His ship, however, remains of use, and the boy, Turlough, shows promise.' The Sontaran grinned horribly. 'You two will remain here and witness my triumph.'

Braast touched a control on his belt, and there was a blaze of energy as he dematerialised.

Tegan turned to the Doctor in despair. 'Doctor, we've got to do something!'

The Doctor said nothing. He was staring out of the window as the Sontaran ship powered up, then swung round to face the fighter craft piloted by Turlough.

The fight was about to commence.

'You understand the controls of the ship?' Braast's eager face stared at Turlough from the screen on the fighter craft's control console.

Turlough nodded. 'Yes, I think so.'

'That is excellent.' The Sontaran paused. 'In case you have any ideas about fleeing, or using this ship to somehow rescue your friends, the robot behind you has been given very clear instructions.'

Braast let his threat hang in the air. Turlough glanced over his shoulder at the robot wrapped round the rear of the pilot's chair, its insect-like mouth clacking frantically.

'I understand,' Turlough said, his mouth dry.

'Then we can begin. I will release control of the fighter craft to you in precisely twenty seconds.' Braast pulled on his helmet and gave a stiff salute. 'For the honour of Sontar!'

The control-console screen went dead.

Turlough gripped the control column of the fighter craft. It was true that he had flown ships of this kind before, but not for an extremely long time. He glanced out at the Sontaran ship hanging malevolently before him. Braast was a trained fighter, a creature bred for war. What chance did Turlough have against a warrior like that?

Unless . . .

A plan began to form in Turlough's brain. It was risky, but it might just work. Then, before he could have any second thoughts, the controls of his ship burst into life.

Tegan and the Doctor watched as Turlough's fighter craft surged forward, on a collision course with Braast's ship. At the last possible moment it pulled up, its cannons blazing with energy.

Taken by surprise at such a bold attack, the Sontaran's craft stood little chance. Energy bolts raked across the spherical hull, cutting huge, ragged gouges in the metal.

'Oh, well played, Turlough!' shouted the Doctor.

Tegan's eyes were wide with astonishment. 'What on earth is he doing?'

'Exactly the opposite of what was expected!' The Doctor turned to her excitedly. 'Braast mistakenly assumed that Turlough would be terrified, that he would do anything to try to avoid a fight. All Sontarans are fundamentally arrogant. They operate like a cat playing with a mouse. The last thing they expect is for the mouse to strike first.'

He turned back towards the window, watching as Turlough's ship arced away into the blackness of space.

'Won't he just make the Sontaran angry?' Tegan asked nervously.

'Oh, I expect he'll be furious!' exclaimed the Doctor. 'But, if Turlough has done enough damage to that ship, then it will give him a distinct advantage.' The Doctor spun round, eyes gleaming with excitement. 'Now, let's see if I can tip the balance a bit more in Turlough's favour!'

Braast struggled to bring the chaos inside his cockpit under control. A dozen small fires spluttered and popped on various control consoles, and the air was thick with acrid smoke. Service robots darted around him, smothering the fires with bursts of extinguishing foam and rerouting circuits from damaged sections.

Braast stabbed savagely at the weapon controls as Turlough's sleek fighter craft swept past him, but none of the automatic targeting systems were working.

'So, our Trion is not as timid as he seems.' Beneath the helmet, Braast's lipless mouth cracked into an unpleasant smile. 'Excellent. My victory will be all the greater.'

Disengaging all the automatic systems, Braast took manual control of the ship, forcing the protesting engines into life. He swung about, and set a course to follow his opponent's craft.

'You want me to do *what?*' Tegan glared at the Doctor.

'Tegan, we don't have a lot of time. Turlough has been lucky so far, but if we don't act quickly –'

'I'm in no mood to have my nervous system scraped again, thank you very much!'

'It is *extremely* unlikely that these robots have any kind of neurological weapons.' The Doctor was starting to get impatient. 'Braast is something of a sadist, as I'm sure you've noticed. If there is any punishment to be meted out, he'll want to do it himself. The worst that's going to happen is that the robots will restrain you.'

'All right, all right.' Tegan held up her hands in resignation. 'Tell me again what the plan is.'

The Doctor nodded at the charred remains of P011Y, which lay on the cargo-bay floor. 'P011Y called itself a Senior Command Automaton. That implies a master positronic override circuit. If I can gain access to that circuit, I should be able to take control of all of Braast's robots.'

'How long will you need?'

'Not long. But you'll have to distract the Sontaran robots to give me time to make the necessary adjustments.'

Tegan sighed unhappily. 'I hope you're right about this, Doctor.'

'Brave heart, Tegan.'

Tegan rolled her eyes. Taking a deep breath, she turned to where the robots were clustered, their gleaming black eyes glinting in the harsh light of the cargo bay.

'Hey! How much longer are you going to keep us here?' As Tegan moved towards them, the robots rose up on their strong metal legs, antennae twitching. 'I demand that you give us food and water.'

One of the robots moved to block her way, but, with a sudden burst of speed, Tegan ducked past it and sprinted towards the TARDIS. There was a sudden flurry of movement as the robots surged after her, clicking furiously.

The Doctor seized his chance. He hurled himself forward, sliding across the floor and coming to a halt next to P011Y's prone remains. Slipping on his glasses, he fumbled with a plate on the robot's metallic torso, pulling it free and peering into the cavity. A box studded with tiny buttons was nestled among a tangle of wires and circuit boards.

'Yes! I thought as much!' The Doctor reached into the cavity, fingers dancing over the tiny controls. 'Now, if I've remembered the codes for Tellurian drives properly . . .'

From behind him, he could hear Tegan shouting in

anger as the robots struggled to restrain her. It would only be a matter of moments before their attention returned to him . . .

'Doctor! Look out!'

A loud metallic skittering told the Doctor that the robots were on their way. He was out of time.

He keyed in the final code and hit the restart command.

Turlough knew that he had exhausted all of his options. Braast had not only managed to catch him, but was matching him move for move, even though his ship must have been crippled. The Sontaran was just too good a pilot. Too good a warrior.

Turlough wrenched the control column to one side as another searing bolt of energy tore past his starboard wing. The fighter craft banked sharply, but Braast was right on his tail. With every desperate move he made to avoid Braast's attacks, the Sontaran got that little bit closer.

'WARNING. WEAPON LOCK.' The console in front of him blared. 'WARNING. WEAPON LOCK. WEAPON LOCK.'

Turlough closed his eyes, waiting for the blast that would finish him off.

But it never came.

'I'm sorry about that, Turlough. You know me – always leaving things to the last minute!'

Turlough opened one eye. 'Doctor?'

'Well, of course!' The Doctor sounded indignant. 'You didn't think I was just going to abandon you, did you?'

It took Turlough a few moments to realise that the Doctor's voice wasn't actually coming from the control console, but from the Sontaran robot behind him.

'How on earth . . .?'

'Access to the command circuit of a Senior Command Automaton,' explained the Doctor. 'I imagine that Braast is equally surprised.'

Braast was more than surprised. He was furious. He had finally got Turlough's fighter craft lined up in his sights and had his finger on the button that would unleash destruction, when everything had gone dead.

He stabbed frantically at the controls. 'Report!' he snarled at the robots around him. 'Explain reason for malfunction!'

'Um, that would be my fault, I'm afraid.'

'What?' Braast growled at the voice booming from the vocal synthesiser of his service robots. 'Is that you, Time Lord?'

'It is. You'll notice that your metal friends are now doing

what I tell them to do –' the Doctor paused mischievously –
'and I've told them to take you back to your fleet. I'm sure
you'll have a splendid time explaining to your commander-in-
chief how you were bested by a boy, a pacifist degenerate and
a worthless human female.'

Braast fumbled with his helmet, feeling a pang of fear for
the first time in his short life.

'No . . . Doctor, you can't!'

'Goodbye, Braast.'

Before the Sontaran could react, the robots activated
the warp drive of his ship. Braast was thrust back into the
padding of his chair by the acceleration, helpless to stop
his ship from carrying him back to his superiors – and the
punishment they would inevitably deal him.

The Doctor let out a deep sigh as the Sontaran ship warped
out of existence in a blaze of ionised particles. 'Good
riddance. Now, let's see what we can do about getting this
freighter back on course.'

A short time later, Turlough emerged through the air lock and
was greeted by a relieved Tegan.

'You had us worried!' She gave him a smile that was
almost admiring. 'Where did you learn to fly like that?'

Turlough shuffled uncomfortably. 'I had a few lessons when I was younger.' He changed the subject quickly. 'Where's the Doctor?'

'Over here, Turlough.' The Doctor's voice rang out from the other side of the cargo bay. Turlough and Tegan wandered over to where he was busily rewiring P011Y's command circuit into the torso of one of the Sontaran robots.

'What a mess!' said Tegan, eyeing the robot distrustfully.

'It's not easy marrying up two completely disparate technologies,' said the Doctor, sounding a bit hurt. 'Nonetheless, I think that I've managed to cobble something together that will last just long enough to get this cargo to the colonists on Loen.'

'Just in time for Christmas?' asked Tegan hopefully.

'Yes!' The Doctor smiled, and patted the Sontaran robot on the top of its silver head. 'Thanks to one of Sontar's little helpers!'

FAIRY TALE OF NEW NEW YORK

Written by Gary Russell

Illustrated by Stewart Easton

The TARDIS landed with a thump, and its doors immediately swung open. Two people strode out of them, as if going for a brisk walk – although the red-headed young woman was a bit brisker than the curly-haired older man behind her.

'Where are we?'

'This, Mel, is the M87 galaxy.'

Melanie Bush looked at the Doctor disdainfully. She did that a lot, because the Doctor got a lot of things wrong – and often tried to talk his way out of it, saying things like, 'I'm not telling you a lie, just a different truth.' That was a particular favourite.

'I thought we were going to M57? To see – and I quote –

"the resplendent veldts that can *only* be seen in that one, unique galaxy".'

The Doctor looked at Mel with a disdain that almost equalled hers. 'I don't like the way you always pretend to remember what I've said word for word.'

'I don't pretend,' Mel retorted. 'I do remember! Memory like –'

'Catkind.'

'Well, I was going to say an elephant.' Mel frowned. The Doctor wasn't really listening, but Mel continued anyway. 'And, besides, this is neither the M87 *nor* the M57 galaxy.' She gestured to the space around them. '*This* appears to be a large metal box.'

'A humming metal box,' the Doctor said, as though correcting her.

Mel crouched down and put her palm to the floor. She was used to answering her own questions about the places she travelled to with the Doctor. The floor was vibrating a little, and Mel smiled as she realised where they must be. 'We're on a ship! A big one, I think.' She glanced around at the dull, industrial-looking space, empty but for one door set into the farthest wall. 'Not a pleasure craft. Probably a dreadnought or something similar.'

The Doctor stood back, leaning casually against the

TARDIS. 'Could be the engine room of an intergalactic liner, or the storage bay of an executive business ship.'

Mel shook her head. 'Not enough Health and Safety signage.'

The Doctor traced his thumbs down the lapels of his multicoloured coat, his left thumb settling on the small cat brooch he always wore.

'Catkind.'

'You said that a moment ago.' Mel glanced back at him.

'Oh, that sharp memory of yours.' He smiled back. 'Amazing retention!'

Mel stood up and walked to the Doctor's side, then gave the cat brooch a tap. 'Why this badge today? I mean, you always wear a cat brooch, but I've never seen this one before.'

'Galaxy M57 is home to the Catkind. I thought wearing this specific brooch might alleviate any potential . . . misunderstandings.'

Mel stared at the brooch. It was the head of a tabby cat wearing what seemed to be a white, winged headdress.

She sighed. 'Doctor, you *just* said we were in M87.'

'M57, M87 – same galaxy, but the number depends on whether you approach it from Galactic Centre or the Great Beyond.'

Mel gave him another of her patented looks: the one

that suggested she didn't believe a word he was saying. 'So, in this particular area of space – wherever it may actually be – *Felis catus* is the dominant species?'

'If you're asking if everyone here is a cat, then no.' The Doctor started to inspect the single doorway leading out of the room, which seemed to be locked. 'But they do have a flourishing socio-economic presence. They run the galaxy's administrative services – police, fire, ambulance, and a pretty significant number of legal firms. All Catkind.'

'I like cats.'

'Just as well.' The Doctor triumphantly, and with more flourish than it deserved, pressed a switch that he'd discovered concealed in the wall. The door slid aside with a hiss of compressed air.

They wandered into the corridor, which to Mel's surprise couldn't have been any more different from the room they'd landed in. Brightly lit, the walls, ceiling and floors somehow seemed to be illuminated from within, giving out a soft, pulsating glow. The Doctor and Mel both felt themselves beginning to relax.

'Soporific,' the Doctor said. 'The Catkind like pumping things into the air.'

Mel nodded, a smile spreading across her face. 'Mmm. I feel a lot calmer already.'

The Doctor walked ahead a little, peered round a junction in the corridor, then hurried back to Mel. 'This way,' he said quietly, turning them both in the opposite direction and beginning to walk quickly.

'Can I help you?' purred a voice behind them.

With a sigh, the Doctor stopped and turned to face the speaker.

Mel did likewise.

Facing them was a cat – but a cat who was human-sized, standing upright, and dressed in a long white smock and a winged headdress. Just like the Doctor's brooch. She was carrying a pile of electronic tablets. The only mark on her crisp white clothing was a small green crescent-shaped badge.

'Hello,' the Doctor said cheerfully. 'Sorry, we got a bit lost. We were trying to find . . . Garfield.'

'I see.' The Catkind tapped at the tablet on top of the pile. 'I'm sorry, but I don't know that name. What department is she in?'

'Dietetics,' the Doctor said. 'Matron Garfield. You must know her – big Catkind, very ginger.'

The Catkind didn't look convinced. She brought up her arm and, as her smock fell away from her arm, revealed a small comms device on her wrist. She tapped at it with a claw from her other paw. 'Novice Shel to Administration. Can you see whether a Matron Garfield is registered in Nutrition and Dietetics?'

'Or possibly Gastroenterology,' the Doctor suggested.

Novice Shel held her paw to her ear, listening to the device. She nodded, then spoke into it again. 'Thank you.'

She suddenly bared all her teeth in a wide smile, causing Mel to take a short step back in surprise. 'We have no record of a Matron Garfield anywhere on New Earth. And she certainly isn't aboard this craft.'

'Doctor –' Mel started to speak, then stopped quickly as the Catkind's eyes widened. She turned to the Doctor.

'You are a doctor, are you?' Novice Shel asked.

With an exaggerated sigh, the Doctor nodded. 'Yes. But I'm not here professionally. Simply a social call. We'll just nip back to our shuttle and –'

Novice Shel looked alarmed. 'You have a shuttle? Parked in a shuttle bay? Have you been through decontamination?'

'Decontamination? Why would we need to –'

Mel looked up at the ceiling, but it was too late – they were suddenly both drenched in a series of colourful and powerful jets of liquid that sprayed down from above. Before either of them could move, a line of three big heater units emerged from the walls on either side of them, blasting them with warm air. The whole process was over in a few seconds.

'Decontamination confirmed,' Novice Shel said, then pointed behind her. 'Admin is down there, on the left. They'll deal with your queries. Good day.'

And Novice Shel went on her way.

Mel glanced at the Doctor – he appeared completely unfazed by their decontamination experience. 'Let's take a look around, shall we?' he suggested.

'Why would we do that?'

'Why not?'

Mel puffed out her cheeks as the Doctor strode off down the corridor. It was going to be one of those days.

After a few minutes of wandering along featureless white corridors, Mel stopped. 'Doctor, why are we *actually* here?'

'Because this is a hospital ship from New Earth. Home of the best and most successful medical care in the nine galaxies.'

'So?'

'So why have they sent a ship into space when they have such wonderful facilities on the planet?'

Mel thought for a second. 'Maybe this is an ambulance.'

'I don't –' the Doctor started to say, before stopping still. He reached down to touch the bright white floor, then the base of the two walls. 'It's warmer here. Designed to be inviting, to make people feel happier than further back, where we met Novice Shel. We must be getting close.'

'To what?'

'I have no idea.'

They turned down the next corridor, and this one was different again: a large green crescent sign on the left wall, and beyond that a huge white door with a window in it. As the Doctor approached, the door slid quietly open.

Mel hurried to join him, and together they walked through it.

They found themselves in a ward. There were about three dozen beds and, next to each bed, what Mel assumed to be state-of-the-art medical equipment. And every bed had a child in it.

'Look at them,' the Doctor said quietly.

They were all humanoid in appearance. A variety of skin tones – Caucasian, Asian, African, plus one that was bright red, one a brilliant white and one lime green.

'Children from across the sector,' he said quietly.

'Problem?' Mel asked.

The Doctor paused. 'Why aren't they being treated on New Earth? The best paediatricians money can buy are down there.'

Another Catkind – this one with fur that, to Mel,

looked just like a Persian blue – suddenly rushed over, a sour expression on her face. 'Who are you?'

'I'm –' the Doctor started.

Just then, one of the children called out excitedly. 'Santa! Look, it's Santa Claus!'

'Father Christmas!' yelled another, clearly overjoyed.

The Doctor swung round, looking behind him. He glanced at Mel. 'Me? Why do they think I'm Santa Claus?'

'Must be the stupid coat.' Mel laughed.

'What do I do now?'

Mel grinned. 'Say "Ho, ho, ho"?'

Before long, the Doctor was quite enjoying being Santa Claus. He entertained the gathered children with some simple magic tricks, finding coins behind their ears and making them vanish again.

Mel was enjoying the sound of laughter – from the Doctor as well as from the children. A very rare thing, to be honest; she couldn't recall the last time she'd seen him this cheerful.

A voice came from just behind her. 'Novice Thelm has just alerted me to your presence in the ward,' it said. 'Who *exactly* are you?'

It was another Catkind, this time with a pure white face,

wearing a green version of the hospital uniform. She looked very much displeased at the disruption to her ward.

'I'm Melanie Bush,' Mel answered truthfully.

'Well, I am Charge Tarrow,' said the nun. 'You should not be here aboard the Abbey.'

Mel thought for a moment. 'The Abbey,' she repeated, before coming to a sudden realisation. 'You're not just nurses – you're nuns!'

'Yes. Sisters of Plenitude. And I repeat: you should not be here. I do not wish to know the hows or whys of your unwanted presence. I would just like you to leave before any more of my Sisters are influenced unduly by you being here.'

Charge Tarrow threw a look towards the Doctor. 'The Children of Receptor may not be corrupted,' she added.

'By laughter and Father Christmas?' Mel scoffed. 'How could that corrupt them?'

Mel saw a flash in Charge Tarrow's eyes. 'Christmas is an Old Earth custom that has no place on New Earth. The children have been taken away from New New York to avoid corruption by such . . . fairy tales and superstitions.'

'Says the nun!' muttered Mel, almost under her breath – but not so quietly that Charge Tarrow couldn't hear.

'Our Order is not structured along any form of theism – just abstention and protection of the human children.'

'Interesting,' Mel said, wondering how much else Charge Tarrow would be willing to tell her. 'I noticed that there are no Catkind children here . . .'

'Our kitlings have special nurseries on New Earth. They do not share the same problems as these children do.'

'Oh. What's wrong with them, exactly? And why are they here? Are they in quarantine?'

Charge Tarrow gave Mel a quizzical look and her whiskers twitched, as if sizing Mel up. 'You truthfully do not know?'

Mel shrugged. 'We're visitors, and we've only just arrived. While His Nibs is playing Santa, it falls to me to fill in the gaps.'

Charge Tarrow sighed. Then she tapped her comms unit. 'Security to the ward, please.' She fixed Mel with a steely glare. 'I'm sorry, but clearly you have docked at the Abbey without clearance.'

'Now, hang on. The TARDIS doesn't dock as such . . .'

Two Catkind in black uniforms stomped into the room. Charge Tarrow pointed a claw at Mel, then towards the Doctor. 'Her, and him. But –' she held her paw up – 'do not alarm the children.'

❄

While Mel was getting herself into trouble with the Catkind, the Doctor had been talking to the children. They all seemed thrilled to see him, which was nice – even though he still didn't think he looked anything like Santa.

He glanced round and saw Mel talking to a Catkind in a green uniform.

A charge nurse, he thought. *Only one down from the matron who presumably runs this hospital.* And the matron, in turn, would be answerable to an abbess, according to the Doctor's understanding of how the Catkind matriarchy worked.

'Are there any other humans on board?' he asked one of the children, a girl aged ten or so named Tasha. The Doctor had deduced that she was a sort of leader to the other kids, probably due to her being one of the eldest. She was also one of the few children not attached by elongated tubes to a variety of machines and plasma bags, so she could move around freely.

Tasha shook her head. 'They won't even let our *parents* visit.'

'Why ever not?'

Tasha shrugged. 'Maybe it's the plague. I reckon we're all carriers.'

'You have a plague?' The Doctor looked at the machines and pumps that the majority of the children were attached to.

'Dunno, but maybe we carry the gene,' Tasha said,

almost repeating herself, as though this was a turn of phrase she'd learned from having heard it over and over again.

'Which plague, Tasha? Do you know its name?'

Tasha reached down to pick up a small electronic tablet attached to the base of the nearest bed. She tapped a few things and a chart appeared on the screen. The Doctor peered at it with interest.

'How silly,' he said. 'There are no medical records here, and certainly nothing about plagues. I think it's time I had a word with the charge nurse over there.'

Tasha grabbed his arm with alarming ferocity. 'No,' she hissed. 'Please, Santa. Don't do that.'

'I'm not really Santa,' he said gently.

'I know,' Tasha replied, with a small smile.

'Call me Doctor instead.' As the words left the Doctor's mouth, he immediately regretted it. Tasha and the other children recoiled.

'I'm not a medical doctor!' he added hurriedly. 'Think of me more as . . . a doctor of fun. Fun with a capital F!'

That didn't seem to reassure the children as much as he'd hoped. But Tasha came back closer. She nodded towards the charge nurse. 'She eats children.'

The Doctor wanted to laugh, but the sincere expression on Tasha's face threw him. 'Really?'

Tasha nodded. 'She's new. She's taken away four kids over the past few weeks, and none of them ever came back. Including my cousin Hector. I think she's had them for Christmas dinner.'

'Boiled,' added a young boy.

'With sprouts,' said another.

'Lots of sprouts. She eats kids and sprouts!' Tasha sat back, as if that explained everything.

The Doctor noticed that Mel was surrounded by security Catkind, and the charge nurse was walking away. One of the Catkind guards looked in his direction and started striding over purposefully.

He patted Tasha's arm. 'I'll be right back.'

The silent Catkind security guard helped the Doctor to his feet with a firm pull and started to lead him away from the children.

'Something interesting to consider, Mel,' the Doctor said, as he was subtly but sharply pushed across the room towards her. 'Why would you need security guards with big guns if this is just a hospital populated by cat nuns and children?'

This was a question they were still contemplating a few moments later, when the Doctor and Mel found themselves facing the abbess. She was a ferocious-looking Catkind in a red version of the nuns' uniform, with additional and rather ornate drapes hanging down from the wimple.

She stared at them over a pair of pince-nez.

'Doctor, Doctor, Doctor. What am I going to do with you?'

The abbess removed her glasses, and wiped them on her uniform. She leaned forward conspiratorially. 'Don't tell Laundry Services that I did that. This ridiculous attire costs almost as much as the whole ship did to build. I have three outfits, each one more uncomfortable than the last, and Laundry Services complain because they have to clean them so often. I have no idea why – I sit here all day, signing documents, reading reports, and then I go to sleep. It's not as if I'm running through service ducts or climbing trees.'

Mel glanced at the Doctor, and there was a glint of something in his eye. He opened his mouth to speak.

'It's there, isn't it, Doctor? On the edge of your mind.'

He held up a hand, wagging a finger as he closed his eyes, trying to remember. 'I'm getting something . . .'

The abbess looked to Mel. 'I'm afraid I didn't catch your name, my dear.'

'Melanie. Melanie Bush . . . um, Your Majesty.'

The abbess suddenly laughed and clapped her paws together. 'Your Majesty! Wonderful. I love that.' Then she smiled broadly. 'You travel with him, yes? From twentieth-century Earth, I imagine? His friends tend to be from there.' She leaned forward. 'Does he still have that robot dog? I never liked the robot dog. Yappy, know-it-all little thing.'

The Doctor gasped. 'I've got it! You're Novice Ayesha!'

'I haven't been a novice for many years, Doctor.'

'The milk vats! The milk vats of New Savannah! That was . . . how long ago *was* that?'

'In my terms, nearly sixty years. In yours, probably a few bodies.'

'Look at you now,' the Doctor said, a smile on his face. 'Abbess of your very own hospital, traversing the spaceways. Not tied to one small planet in one small part of the galaxy. Just like you always wanted.'

'I owe my sense of wanderlust to the Doctor,' the abbess told Mel.

'I know the feeling,' Mel replied, nodding.

'I'm pleased for you, Ayesha,' the Doctor went on. 'What a lot you've accomplished!'

Then his expression abruptly changed. He narrowed his eyes, suspicion flooding his face as he stared at the abbess.

'Here you are now, keeping human children in a sealed hospital in space, with armed security guards to protect you. From what? A bunch of ten-year-olds who want nothing

A squat figure clad in jet-black armour and wearing a gleaming domed helmet materialised in front of them. The figure was flanked by a squad of angular metallic robots, each of which appeared poised to attack at any moment.

Sontar's Little Helpers

Written by Mike Tucker

Illustrated by Staffan Gnosspelius

*'I think it's high time we introduced the Catkind to the joy
of Christmas, once and for all.'*

Fairy Tale of New New York

Written by Gary Russell

Illustrated by Stewart Easton

There was the creature, its large body swathed in a voluminous red cloak trimmed with white fur, the hood pulled up. It had a canvas bag tightly gripped in one enormous paw.

The Grotto

Written by Mike Tucker

Illustrated by Charlie Sutcliffe

What confronted him under the paper was a simple, glowing cube, small enough to fit quite neatly in the palm of his hand. It pulsed with brilliant white light and seemed to weigh almost nothing. The Doctor could hear it whispering to him.

Ghost of Christmas Past

Written by Scott Handcock

Illustrated by Jennifer Skemp

more than a visit from Santa Claus, most of whom are tied to centrifuges draining their blood for who knows what purpose?' He gave a short, hollow laugh. 'Yes, I'm *so* happy for you. You've become a shadow of who you used to be.'

Mel was aghast. 'Hold on, Doctor. I thought she was your friend?'

'No, Mel. *You* hold on. And you, Ayesha – or Abbess, or whatever nonsensical title you've found yourself adopting.'

'My, haven't you grown hot-headed in your old age? I'm not sure I'd be so quick to throw around accusations of adopting nonsensical titles if I were you, Doctor,' said the abbess. She seemed more amused than angry. 'Please do tell me. Who exactly is this Santa Claus?'

'Father Christmas,' offered Mel.

The abbess looked at her blankly. 'I have never understood what this Christmas thing the children talk about is. Perhaps you could enlighten me?'

'Not now,' the Doctor interrupted. 'Something more important to address first. Apparently one of your charge nurses is eating human children. Right under your nose!'

Even Mel thought that sounded a bit unlikely.

The Doctor coughed. 'At least that's what the children think. I'm sure there's a more logical explanation.'

'You presumably mean Charge Tarrow?' the abbess

said thoughtfully. 'Children don't like change, do they? They don't trust it. Tarrow only joined us a few weeks ago, and I think perhaps she lacks the bedside manner needed to deal with human children.' The abbess leaned back in her chair. 'Doctor, Mel – why do you think the humans on New Earth like us?'

'You tend not to eat them?' suggested the Doctor.

'Humans like cats,' Mel said quietly. 'They make good pets.'

'Patronising, but absolutely true,' said the abbess. 'And that's why the Sisters of Plenitude took over the medical profession. The majority of humans find being in hospital an unpleasant experience. If the hospital staff are of a species which they are conditioned to relax around, it makes them better patients.'

'A number of humans don't like cats at all,' the Doctor said. 'The Handcock Hypothesis states that –'

'Yes, well, there are a number of Catkind who don't like fleshy humans either, Doctor, but we live in a multicultural universe. We learn to make the things that separate us also unite us.'

The Doctor paused. 'What are you doing to the children?'

'Do you know the main cause of antagonism between Catkind and humans?'

Mel answered immediately. 'Allergies. To fur.'

The abbess smiled. 'I see you still choose your companions well, Doctor. Always one step ahead of you.'

'I was about to say that, actually,' the Doctor said, clearly irked. 'So, let me see. You want to live in harmony with the humanoids on New Earth, which means you need to defeat allergies.' He clicked his fingers. 'These children are not allergic, and you are trying to synthesise the qualities which make them so.'

'At which point we will devise a way to inject that unique antihistamine safely into the atmosphere of the planet, allowing allergic humans to live far more pleasant lives.' The abbess spread her paws wide. 'Simple.'

'And that's why you won't let their parents aboard. To avoid contamination or false results.' The Doctor nodded. 'Have you told the children that?'

'Told them what?'

'The reason they're here. They're all under the impression that things are far more sinister. They think they've got the plague! Give them an early Christmas present, Ayesha. Tell them the truth.'

The abbess looked confused. 'We've kept nothing back from the children. At least, we've always kept their parents fully informed.'

Mel snorted derisively. 'Oh, parents don't tell their kids anything useful like that!'

At this, the abbess appeared truly surprised. 'We tell our kitlings everything.'

'Adult humans are different, Ayesha. They can't be trusted to remember important things,' said the Doctor. 'They haven't had millennia of civilisation to grow up like the Catkind. In my experience, their parenting skills can vary wildly, from overprotective to downright useless. Just tell the children what's going on, to their faces! Allay their fears! That way, you'll have calmer children who are capable of producing more of the natural antihistamine you need. And then you can send them home.'

The Catkind looked from the Doctor to Mel and back again. 'I cannot believe . . . I never . . . No one told me they were distressed!'

'I'd be distressed if I was tied into a hospital monitor, not knowing why, unable to see my mum and dad,' Mel said cautiously. 'Especially if I thought that Charge Tarrow was eating my friends.'

'Tasha told me that four of her friends were taken by Tarrow and hadn't come back.'

The abbess opened her mouth to reply, but then tapped the comms device on her arm instead. A Catkind security guard walked in and bowed deeply to her.

'And another thing –' the Doctor started, but the abbess silenced him with a wave.

'Bring Charge Tarrow to us immediately, please.'

The guard promptly walked back out.

'You wanted to know why we need guards, Doctor. I have two words for you: Space. Pirates.' The abbess sighed, seeming almost exhausted. 'There are slavers, corsairs and general ne'er-do-wells out here in space, many of whom would see a group of human children as valuable bounty. Or as excellent slaves. Hence our security guards.'

The door opened again and Charge Tarrow came in, looking darkly at the Doctor and Mel, before bowing graciously to her abbess. Ayesha swiftly recounted what Tasha had told the Doctor and asked for an explanation.

Charge Tarrow hung her head low. 'I'm sorry, Abbess. I have done you a great disservice.'

The abbess sighed again, as the Doctor and Mel stared. 'I think you had better tell us everything.'

An hour later, the Doctor and Mel were in a different part of the Abbey: the ship's living quarters. Walking beside them were Charge Tarrow, Novice Shel and a number of other Sisters of Plenitude.

Abbess Ayesha was there too, attended by a couple of novices who seemed most distressed that, by walking the corridors, her attire might get dirty.

'We are in a sterile atmosphere,' she scolded them gently. 'I *wish* there was some dirt in the corridors. It might justify the Abbey's cleaning bills.'

Also with them were Tasha and a handful of the other human children – those who were able to move away from their machines and centrifuges. Excitingly, they had now been joined by their four missing friends, including Tasha's cousin Hector. Mel would never forget the gleeful expressions on their faces when they had been reunited.

They were all here to look at something quite unorthodox. Enough for Charge Tarrow to be racked with guilt and sorrow, her grouchy demeanour clearly compensation for the fact she knew she had done something wrong.

Mel eased her way through the group to see what the fuss was about.

Charge Tarrow had turned her living quarters into a smaller version of the children's ward. In it were three young kitlings, looking a bit scared themselves, eyes like saucers, whiskers and tails twitching.

Pushing gently past Mel, Hector went to sit with the

kitlings, all of whom moved to hug him.

Mel looked at the Doctor. 'All right, so everyone's safe. Clearly some kind of Christmas miracle! But I'm still not sure what's going on.'

The Doctor pointed at the machinery the kitlings were attached to.

'They're just like the machines Tasha and her friends had in the ward.'

The Doctor nodded. 'Ten out of ten, Mel.' He turned his attention to his old friend, the abbess. 'It never occurred to you that allergies worked both ways?'

Ayesha shook her head, nearly causing her pince-nez to fall from her nose – although one of the novices already had a paw out to catch them if they did.

The abbess stepped forward and addressed Charge Tarrow. 'If you had told me what you were doing, I would have helped.'

Charge Tarrow shook her head. 'The Abbey's mission – the reason the Sisters are here – is to help the humans to overcome their allergies to us. But these kitlings, from my own family, are allergic to *humans*.'

The Doctor nodded. 'So you've been reverse-engineering the human children's natural antihistamine, to develop something similar for Catkind.'

'It is a rare affliction for a kitling to be born with, Doctor,' Charge Tarrow said sadly. 'But a devastating one.'

The abbess looked at Charge Tarrow, then at the Doctor. 'It would seem, Doctor, that this hospital is required to expand its horizons,' she said. 'It's funny how whenever I am around you I always find my horizons are expanded.'

She moved towards Charge Tarrow and placed an arm round her shoulders. 'We will work together to find the cure – for the sake of these kitlings, and for the humans they might one day grow up to treat.'

Mel smiled as Charge Tarrow beamed, relieved to have shared her secret with the abbess at last.

'I think,' the Doctor said, 'I might need to expand another horizon while I'm here.' He unclipped the cat brooch, which Mel now understood showed a Sister of Plenitude, from his coat lapel. Stepping across the floor of the makeshift ward, he presented it to Tasha.

'Now that Charge Tarrow's secret is out in the open, I think it's high time we introduced the Catkind to the joy of Christmas, once and for all.'

With that, the Doctor led Tasha away, speaking animatedly of Christmas trees, presents, carolling – and how exactly they might cook a Christmas dinner all the way up here in space . . .

THE GROTTO

Written by Mike Tucker

Illustrated by Charlie Sutcliffe

A ce took a deep breath and gazed from where she stood on the roof of Macy's department store out across the snowy streets of New York. To her immense satisfaction, the city looked exactly as she had hoped it would – a forest of towering skyscrapers and skinny tenement buildings, lights blazing from every window, wide avenues stretching out in a neatly ordered grid, echoing with the sound of police sirens. A few blocks away, the lights from Times Square flashed and oscillated in a seemingly never-ending sequence, and the illuminated spire of the Empire State Building lit up the low clouds that hung around it like a shroud.

The entire city was blanketed in a thick carpet of snow, and great mounds of slush and ice were piled on the pavements. *Or, rather, the sidewalks,* Ace mentally corrected herself.

She was impressed. If this much snow had fallen on London, the entire place would have ground to a halt. Although, come to think of it, if only a few *millimetres* of snow fell on London, it would still likely grind to a halt.

She watched a couple emerge from a bar on the street below, then hurry off into the freezing night, coats and scarves pulled tight. Huge clouds of white steam billowed from vents in the glistening streets. Ace grinned. It was just like she'd seen in the movies. Cautiously she peered a little further out over the edge of the roof, craning her neck to see if there actually *were* any cops eating doughnuts on the street corners.

'Ace!' The Doctor's voice rang out from the other side of the roof. 'Be careful.'

'I'm only looking, Professor.'

Ace hopped down from the parapet, and glanced across to where the Doctor was hunched over a large grey metal shape, prodding and poking at it with the tip of his umbrella. A gust of icy wind swirled across the roof. Pulling her bomber jacket tight round her, Ace trudged towards him, taking a childish satisfaction in the crunching, squeaking sound that her footfalls made in the snow.

She looked over the Doctor's shoulder at the thing he was studying.

'It's an escape pod, isn't it?'

'Yes.' The Doctor didn't look up.

'Well, that's good then, isn't it? I mean, good that something escaped?'

'Possibly . . .'

Ace rolled her eyes. The Doctor was obviously in one of those moods where he was going to be mysterious.

They had been in orbit round Earth when they had first detected the spacecraft. The Doctor had set his hearts on showing Ace the aurora borealis from space, so had materialised the TARDIS in hover mode over the northern hemisphere, promising Ace the best Christmas-light display of her life. Then, he had opened up the scanner screen, and tuned the TARDIS receivers into an American radio station that was playing nothing but Christmas music. He and Ace spent a few happy minutes bopping around the console room and watching the incredible display of shifting, shimmering lights wrapping round the planet below.

Ace should have guessed it would be too good to last.

It was the Doctor who had first spotted the spacecraft – an arrow of silver amid the swirling colours. Darting to the console, he had trained the scanner on the mysterious vessel, and he and Ace had watched as it arced towards the surface of Earth.

His face had turned grim. 'They're not going to like that down there, are they?'

Leaning forward over the console, he had tuned the TARDIS receivers into a different frequency; the festive songs were replaced by the sound of the North American Aerospace Defense Command. As they listened, American voices began light-heartedly joking about Santa being early . . . but their tone soon changed to one of horror as the realisation of an actual alien incursion hit home.

Ace had closed her eyes when the order to fire missiles had come; she had then despaired at her species when the whoops and cheers that confirmed a direct hit echoed around the TARDIS console room.

The Doctor had leaped into action, tracking the path of the stricken spacecraft and sending the TARDIS spinning after it.

That had been ten minutes ago, and now the only thing left of the alien spacecraft was this escape pod, crashed on the roof of Macy's.

A sudden thought struck Ace. 'Hey, Professor, why didn't it smash right through the roof?'

'Because of these.' The Doctor tapped the curved metal

vanes protruding from one side of the pod. 'Gravitational dampeners. They created an inverse gravity spiral, slowing the pod's descent from orbit, whereas these –' he tapped another series of odd-looking protuberances – 'created a jamming shield so that no one could track its trajectory.' He looked smug. 'No one who isn't me, that is.'

'So the people who shot it down –'

'Don't know that it's here. No.'

'Which just leaves us with one question.' Ace looked around the empty expanse of the roof. 'Where is our survivor?'

The Doctor turned and pointed at a series of large footprints in the snow. Decidedly inhuman footprints. 'Shall we go and find out?' he asked, with a small smile.

Ace and the Doctor followed the trail of footprints through a jumble of air conditioners and satellite dishes. The trail ended at a fire exit, where the thick metal door had been ripped from its hinges.

'Something tells me that our survivor might not be all that friendly, Professor,' said Ace, nervously peering through the open doorway and into the darkened stairwell beyond.

The Doctor frowned. 'Let's not be hasty, Ace. They might just have wanted to get out of the cold.' He ran his hand across one of the deep gashes in the metal door. 'Let's not assume the worst until –'

Before the Doctor could finish his sentence, a blood-curdling howl rang out from the lightless stairwell. The howl was followed almost immediately by a terrified scream, a couple of gunshots and then silence.

Ace turned to the Doctor with a sigh. 'Until it actually happens.'

The Doctor and Ace crept slowly down the dark stairwell, trying to make as little sound as possible on the metal treads. Since the scream, there had been nothing but silence from below.

They reached a landing and found yet another door ripped from its hinges. Keeping Ace behind him, the Doctor peered cautiously into the space beyond.

'Can you see anything?' whispered Ace.

'It's difficult to see, but it looks like we're in . . .' His voice trailed off as he stepped through the doorway. 'A forest.'

'Eh?'

Puzzled, Ace hurried after the Doctor, then stopped in astonishment. He was right – it *was* a forest! Row upon row of trees stretched off in every direction. As her eyes became accustomed to the low light, Ace realised that they

were artificial trees, their plastic boughs festooned with every
type of ornament imaginable. Ace had never seen so many
Christmas trees in one place.

'Wicked!'

As she moved forward to get a closer look, the toe of
her boot knocked against something small and metallic.
She looked down. Bullet casings, next to a dark patch of
something else.

Blood.

'Doctor . . .'

The Doctor came to her side, and stooped down to
examine it more closely.

'Is it . . .?'

'Human?' The Doctor picked up a plastic nametag from
the floor – the ID for a security firm. The laminated plastic
encased the photo of a young, fair-haired man. The Doctor
read out the name. 'Harvey Meeker.'

'Why is it doing this?' Ace felt a sudden ripple of anger.
'Whatever this creature is, it must be intelligent. Why is it
being so aggressive?'

'I'm not sure, but – aha.'

Something else had caught the Doctor's eye: a glint
of burnished metal half buried in the artificial snow that
carpeted the floor. He snatched it up, brushing off the plastic

flakes and examining it intently. His face fell.

'Oh no.'

'What's wrong, Professor?'

The Doctor held the object out for Ace to see. It was a slim curve of what looked like silver metal, its surface etched with a tracery of delicate patterns. Thin wires and tiny connectors hung from one side, the ends tinged with dark fluid.

Ace looked at the Doctor quizzically. 'Is it an implant of some kind?'

'Very good.' The Doctor nodded approvingly. 'A neural inhibitor, to be exact. A behaviour modifier.' He sighed. 'I had my suspicions as to what we were chasing, and this confirms it.'

Ace waited for the Doctor to go on. 'And?' she prompted.

'It's a Stellogratt, a predator from the forest world of Veltt. Savage, ruthless, an efficient hunter.' He looked around the darkened store nervously. 'It's operating on its most basic instinct. To find warmth, shelter –' he glanced down at the picture on the ID card – 'and food.'

Ace shook her head. 'I don't get it. The implant and the escape pod are both pretty sophisticated pieces of technology for a forest hunter.'

The Doctor sighed. 'The Stellogratt are an artificially

enhanced species. Their planet was an important staging post in an interstellar war between the Elayyn and the K'rin. The K'rin forces were badly depleted, so their scientists took animals from the jungles of Veltt and turned them into bionic weapons, using implants and surgery to bring their minds up to a point where they could be useful as soldiers, but retained their hunting instincts and savagery.'

'But the implant has been busted.' Ace indicated the sliver of metal in the Doctor's hand.

'Yes. A lucky shot from Mr Meeker, most likely.'

'So the Stellogratt has reverted to its natural state?'

The Doctor nodded. 'Yes. A hunter.' He peered through the artificial forest. 'And in here it will have a distinct advantage.'

'Well, if we can't reason with it, we're just going to have to capture it, aren't we? A place like this is bound to have a sports section. We could get ourselves some hockey nets or something.' Ace's face lit up. 'Hey! I might even find myself a new baseball bat!'

'No, no, no!' The Doctor waggled his hands at Ace in irritation. 'Trying to take on a Stellogratt in single combat is an appallingly dangerous idea.'

'Then what are we going to do, Professor? We can't just leave it here. Someone else is going to get hurt!'

The Doctor thought for a moment, then spoke quietly. 'We need a way of confusing and disorientating it.'

Ace snorted. 'Confuse and disorientate it. Right. Why don't you just talk to it? That should do the job.'

'Ace . . .' The Doctor's tone left her in no doubt that he wasn't in the mood for levity.

'Then what are we going to do?'

'I'm thinking.'

The Doctor turned slowly in a circle, tapping the handle of his umbrella against his lips. Suddenly his eyes widened as he spotted something. 'Aha! The very thing.' He set off through the artificial trees. Ace hurried after him.

When she caught up with him, he was standing in front of a large store map, which was bolted to the wall next to the elevators.

'That's what we're after!' He stabbed the tip of his umbrella at the map.

Ace squinted at the words he was pointing at. 'The perfume department?'

'Yes.'

Ace frowned. 'Hardly the time to do your Christmas shopping, Professor.'

The Doctor leaned close and whispered conspiratorially. 'The Stellogratt has a highly developed sense of smell, which it uses to hunt its prey. If we can overload that sense of smell . . .'

'You want to throw stink bombs at it?' Ace was incredulous.

'Exactly!' The Doctor beamed at her. 'Now, I want you to go down to the perfume department and grab as many bottles as you can carry.'

'Hang on a minute, Professor. Are you sure that splitting up is the right thing to do?'

'I don't have time to argue with you, Ace!' snapped the Doctor. 'I'll see if I can track the creature to its lair. I'll meet you back here in ten minutes.'

Ace nodded. 'All right. Whatever you say.'

'And, Ace –' he fixed her with a steely glare – 'be careful. No stupid risks.'

Ace grinned at him. 'Of course not!'

She ran off towards the escalators. The Doctor watched as she vanished into the darkness.

'I'll be taking enough of those myself,' he muttered.

Ace bounded down one of the escalators, taking the steps two or three at a time. It was an old-fashioned wooden escalator; she was surprised to see one still in New York's best-known department store. Ace was transported back to her childhood, and memories of riding the clacking, rickety escalators on the

London Underground with her grandmother. They had all been replaced in the 1980s after the King's Cross fire . . .

But this wasn't the time to let her mind wander. She needed to concentrate. She would be no help to the Doctor if she ran into some trigger-happy security guard and got stuck down here.

Refocusing, Ace counted down each landing that she came to. Floor five, floor four, floor three, floor two . . . She almost missed the floor that she was aiming for, only remembering at the last moment that Americans called the ground floor the first floor.

Breathlessly she emerged into the spacious showroom, her nose wrinkling at the smell of hundreds of different kinds of perfume and aftershave. Like the top floor, the entire place was festooned with Christmas decorations. They certainly didn't do anything by halves on this side of the Atlantic.

Snatching up a couple of Macy's shopping bags, Ace started grabbing bottle after bottle of perfume from the displays.

The Doctor made his way cautiously through the forest of artificial trees. After passing through a large section of metallic reds, blues and silvers, the gaudy colours finally gave way and the Doctor found himself surrounded by trees of a more realistic, but not quite natural, green.

He had hoped to have picked up some sign of the Stellogratt by now, but he had underestimated just how extensive the Macy's Christmas-tree display was. It was the perfect environment for the creature to hide in.

He stopped, head cocked to one side, listening for any sound of movement. A rhyme popped into his head. *'Twas the night before Christmas, when all through the house, not a creature was stirring, not even a* –

There was a sudden noise a short distance away. The rustle of something moving through the fake trees. Pushing apart the branches in front of him, the Doctor stared ahead in disbelief.

There was the creature, its large body swathed in a voluminous red cloak trimmed with white fur, the hood pulled up. It had a canvas bag tightly gripped in one enormous paw. As the Doctor watched, the Stellogratt stopped, letting the bag drop to the floor, and pulled back its hood.

The Doctor grimaced. Stellogratts could hardly be described as the most attractive species at the best of times, but this was a particularly brutish example. A thick, gorilla-like brow jutted over red-rimmed eyes, thick folds of grey flesh bristled with coarse hair, and rows of razor-sharp teeth gnashed together as the creature tentatively sniffed at the air with a quivering, bat-like nose.

The Doctor looked around for somewhere to hide. Just a short distance away was a cashier counter festooned with tinsel and stuffed animals. He darted forward, ducking behind the wooden desk as the Stellogratt pushed on through the Christmas trees. The Doctor held his breath and hunched down among the soft toys. If the creature detected him now, that would be it.

But the Stellogratt suddenly gave a grunt of pain, then raised a clawed paw to its head. Peering through the antlers of a large, cuddly reindeer, the Doctor could see a swathe of raw, red flesh glinting on the creature's scalp, and the gleam of scarred metal. The unfortunate security guard's shot had clearly impacted directly on the neural-inhibitor implant, ripping it free. A combination of that and the trauma of the crash-landing had obviously left the creature in a confused and weakened state.

As the Doctor watched, the Stellogratt snatched up its bag again and shambled off through the trees like some monstrous Santa Claus.

The Doctor stared after it thoughtfully. 'Now just where did you get those clothes?' he murmured to himself.

He looked back in the direction from which the creature had come, and a sign hanging above the treetops caught his eye. Welcome to Santaland! it said, in bright red type. Come and meet Santa in his grotto!

'Ah, a grotto.' The Doctor nodded. 'Yes, I suppose that would be ideal.'

Extracting himself from his hiding place, he set off through the artificial forest once more, following a trail of signs designed to build the excitement of children as they drew closer to Santa.

Almost there!

Can you hear him yet?

Have you been naughty or nice?

All the signs did now was make the Doctor more apprehensive.

Abruptly the Doctor found himself in an artificial forest glade. What had once been a neat line of railings designed to keep children and parents in an orderly line was now a pile of twisted metal. The bodies of fibreglass elves lay in deep piles of artificial snow, their smiling heads detached by savage blows. On the far side of the clearing, a small cabin constructed from candy canes had been torn open as something large had pushed its way inside.

The Doctor hurried across the clearing and peered inside the structure. He had a hunch that the creature might be hiding something rather precious inside its candy-cane hideout. He needed to act quickly if he was going to get in and out before the Stellogratt returned.

'Mr Meeker?' he hissed into the dark cabin. 'Are you there?'

There was nothing but silence from inside. With a final glance over his shoulder the Doctor clambered into the cabin, pushing aside splintered fibreglass and dangling tinsel.

The interior of the cabin was tinged with a musty animal smell, which the Doctor was certain was not part of the intended Christmas-grotto experience. Walls designed to guide children along a meandering, winding path had been roughly pushed aside to create a long central passageway. Gingerly, the Doctor made his way forward, using his umbrella as a support to keep his balance on the uneven floor.

The crude tunnel emerged into a chamber festooned with tinsel garlands and dominated by a large golden chair with scarlet upholstery. Slumped next to it was the body of a young man in uniform. The Doctor hurried over, placing his umbrella on the floor and taking the young man's pulse.

Thankfully, he was alive.

'Mr Meeker!' The Doctor gently shook the young man by the shoulders, wincing as he caught sight of a livid bruise on his forehead.

Meeker's eyes fluttered. 'Wha . . . What . . .?' He jerked

awake, pulling away from the Doctor in panic. 'No! Get away from me!'

The Doctor quickly clamped his hand across the young man's mouth. 'Quiet, or you're going to get us both killed! Do you understand?'

Meeker's eyes were wild and frightened, but he nodded slowly.

'Good.' The Doctor took his hand away.

'Who are you?' whispered Meeker, his voice wavering. 'And what was that thing?'

'I'm the Doctor, and I promise I will explain everything, but right now we need to get away from here, as quickly and as quietly as possible. Can you walk?'

'I think so.'

'Good.' The Doctor snatched up his umbrella. 'Then follow me.'

The Doctor led the way back through the ragged passageway, until they were on the deserted shop floor once more, in the clearing in front of the cabin. He paused for a moment, listening, then turned to the security guard, his face grim. 'From this point on it is essential that you remain absolutely silent, OK?'

No sooner had the words left his lips than the sound of loud and tuneless singing rang out through the darkness.

'*Jingle bells, jingle bells, jingle all the way! Oh, what fun it is to ride on a one-horse open sleigh . . .*'

The Doctor spun in horror to see an elderly man in a janitor's coat emerging through the trees. The Doctor waved frantically at him, desperate to attract his attention and make him stop singing.

But the man had already stopped. He was staring in amazement at the devastated Christmas grotto.

'What in the name of –'

The words died in his throat as the Stellogratt, still dressed in its Santa robes, burst into the clearing and let out a shattering roar.

Ace had almost finished filling her shopping bags with perfume bottles when the roar echoed down the escalators. Even coming from several floors above, the sound of the Stellogratt was terrifyingly loud.

Ace went pale. 'Oh no . . .'

Snatching up the bags, she raced for the escalators.

The Stellogratt pushed its way back inside the grotto, dragging Meeker and the terrified janitor by their clothes, oblivious to their cries of pain as they were hauled roughly over the shattered walls. The creature had slung the Doctor under one massive arm, and he hung there like a rag doll in the grip of some huge, fearsome child.

'Please! You must listen to me. I'm here to help you!' The Doctor struggled weakly, desperate to make himself understood, but the creature just snarled at him.

Lumbering into the chamber where it had made its nest, it dropped the Doctor unceremoniously in a heap on the floor and released the two other men. Then, it slumped into the ornate chair, glaring at them balefully and sliding its pink tongue over its gleaming teeth.

Meeker was trying to calm down the almost hysterical janitor. 'Byron, you've gotta stop panicking!'

Byron was staring with wild eyes at the thing sitting on the chair. 'But it's a monster, Harvey! A real-life monster!'

'Quiet! Both of you!' The Doctor's voice cut across them like a thunderclap.

Both men fell silent. The Doctor clambered to his feet, then turned to face the Stellogratt, fixing it with a piercing gaze.

'Listen to me.' His voice was low, hypnotic. 'Somewhere inside your head is the memory of the intelligence that you once had. You have been in a crash. An accident. Your implant has been damaged. I can fix it. I can help.'

The Doctor slowly withdrew the implant from his jacket

pocket. The creature's eyes flicked down and fixed on the gleaming metal.

'Do you understand anything that I am saying? *You need my help.*'

A guttural growl built in the creature's chest and deep, slurring words spilled from its lips. 'I remember . . .'

'Yes?' The Doctor's voice was urgent, encouraging.

'I remember the hunt. The scent of blood, of prey. I remember the forests, the calls of my people.'

'But that was before. Do you remember the war? New life was given to you. New understanding.'

The creature snarled. 'I remember war. And pain. And death.' It slumped back in the chair. 'But that is all past. Now all I feel is cold and tired. And . . .'

'Yes?' The Doctor leaned closer. 'What else do you feel?'

The creature's huge mouth opened wide in a terrifying smile. 'Hungry!'

The Doctor stumbled back in horror as enormous paws tipped with razor-sharp claws reached out for him.

A familiar voice boomed from the end of the passageway. 'Professor! Incoming!'

The Doctor barely had time to duck before the first of the perfume bottles crashed into the wall behind him and shattered. As he scrambled out of the way, a barrage of different-coloured bottles rained down on the furious Stellogratt; as each one landed and broke, the cramped space filled with an increasingly overpowering scent.

The Doctor scrabbled for his umbrella, snapping it open as protection against the flying glass and splashing perfume. He could see Meeker and Byron cowering in the corner, arms thrown up over their heads.

The Stellogratt thrashed and roared, trying to bat away the glass missiles – but Ace's aim was too good, and in seconds the creature was drenched in perfume.

The Doctor peered round the edge of his umbrella, desperate to see if his theory had proved correct, but his eyes were starting to stream from the over-perfumed atmosphere. His breath was catching in his throat. He could hear coughs and splutters from Meeker and Byron as they also struggled to breathe. *Surely all this must be affecting the Stellogratt too?*

Almost on cue, the creature's furious roars started to falter. Through watering eyes, the Doctor saw it begin to weave and stagger. As yet another perfume bottle smashed against its body, the Stellogratt gave a strangled cry and collapsed with a crash that shook the remaining walls of the grotto.

Unsteadily, the Doctor crunched his way through the shattered glass that now littered the floor, to the corner where

Meeker and Byron crouched. With the security guard's help, they managed to get the elderly janitor to his feet and out of the suffocating grotto.

Ace was standing outside, tossing one remaining bottle of perfume from hand to hand. 'Did you see that, Professor? Every one a direct hit!' She grinned. 'I should be playing for the New York Yankees.'

The Doctor coughed, wiping perfume from his hair with a large paisley-patterned handkerchief. 'I've always been a Brooklyn Cyclones man, myself.'

Ace peered inside the ruined grotto at the unconscious Stellogratt. 'It worked then?'

'Yes.' The Doctor sniffed the reeking handkerchief in distaste and stuffed it back into his pocket. 'And now we need to get our sleeping friend back to the TARDIS as quickly as possible, so that I can reattach the neural-inhibitor implant and get him home.'

Ace frowned. 'But how on earth are we going to move him?'

'I can probably help with that.' Byron shuffled forward nervously. 'There's a couple of carts in the basement big enough to move that . . . thing.' He shrugged. 'It's the least I can do, given that you saved my life.'

'Splendid!' said the Doctor cheerfully. 'Perhaps Mr Meeker can give you a hand?'

For a moment the security guard looked as though he was going to argue, but the Doctor fixed him with the same piercing stare that he had used on the Stellogratt. All the questions and uncertainty quickly vanished from Meeker's face. 'Right you are, Doctor.'

As the two men hurried away to get the trolley, Ace sniffed the Doctor's jacket. 'Sorry, Professor. I've made a bit of a mess of your jacket.'

'That's all right, Ace.' The Doctor grinned at her. 'I think you'll find that perfume is a very traditional gift at Christmas.'

GHOST OF
CHRISTMAS PAST

Written by Scott Handcock

Illustrated by Jennifer Skemp

The Doctor wrenched himself up from the floor of the TARDIS console room. Sparks rained down from the girders above, and the Cloister Bell tolled ominously.

This isn't good, he thought, as his fingers danced across the controls.

The TARDIS was caught in a bout of temporal turbulence, caused by a fight on the fringes of the Time War. It had only been a local skirmish – a petty squabble between a handful of the Temporal Powers – but in the current climate that was enough to cause terrible repercussions.

History was in flux across the cosmos, as it had been ever since the Time War started. The Time Lords turned their attentions away from governing established history and protecting the Web of Time, and instead threw all their resources into battling the Daleks and their allies.

There would be casualties on both sides. Worse still, other races would become embroiled in the crossfire. Entire civilisations might cease to exist as errant timelines clashed and overwrote each other. For a time traveller, this made life more than a little complicated.

Of course, the Doctor had never intended to get involved in this fight in the first place. He'd simply been passing through, trying to help in whatever way possible. When the fighting broke out, he'd tried to save whoever he could – but to no avail.

History had already begun to rewrite itself around him. Timelines had started to shift, reimagining both the future and the past. Those the Doctor had managed to rescue had never been born, and so he'd been left with no one to save.

Suddenly something struck the TARDIS hard. The Doctor cried out, clinging to the console for support.

The TARDIS had collided with two conflicting timelines, the console told him, and was now ensnared between the two opposing strands. Neither timeline could yet claim dominance over the other, nor could they be reconciled – and the TARDIS was tearing itself apart as it tried to process this.

There was nowhere left to go, the Doctor realised. He was caught deep within the maelstrom of the vortex. And he could feel the TARDIS's pain – its engines were groaning in frustration, desperately searching for a time track, and a sickly yellow glow had begun to spill from the central column.

The Doctor had little choice. He had to get away, whatever the cost.

He darted round the console, flicking switches on all six panels. Then he slammed the brake down hard and braced himself as they free-fell back into real time, dropping from the vortex like a stone . . .

When the Doctor eventually woke up, he was still in one piece. To his great relief, so was the TARDIS. He hauled himself on to the console and stumbled over to the destination read-outs.

HUMANIAN ERA

EARTH

24 DECEMBER – 11:59:59 – 2016

The Doctor smiled. It was Christmas Eve!

Then his smile faltered. Christmas was traditionally a time for loved ones, for friends and family. He had once had so many of both, before the Time War began.

But now?

Christmas would just be a day like any other.

He sighed and threw open the scanner, watching as the cavernous roof began to shimmer with colour. A swirling spacescape formed, projected from the girders arching over him – and there, at the centre of the image, was the small blue-green planet he cared for so much.

'Earth,' the Doctor sighed. He watched as it turned peacefully on its axis, suspended against the vast, black expanse of space. *How long since I last visited Earth?* he wondered.

Suddenly energised, the Doctor began to whirl round the console, flicking at switches and calibrating the controls for an impromptu trip to the planet below.

Satisfied, he slammed the final lever . . .

And nothing happened.

'That's odd,' the Doctor muttered, checking the console. 'We're not moving!'

He rattled the brake handle, just to be certain.

'*Very* odd,' he said, scratching his head.

The monitor insisted they were held in a temporal orbit, but nothing else untoward. The Doctor double-checked the read-outs, triple-checked his materialisation settings – everything he could think of, trying to determine what might have happened.

Nothing. No faults had been recorded. The TARDIS had simply stopped.

Perhaps she's just exhausted, thought the Doctor.

They'd both been through so much in the last few months – if it even *was* months. It was hard to tell any more. Time Lords often struggled with the passage of time, but especially so when travelling alone, without anyone to help keep track.

Stuck in a time loop in the final second of Christmas Eve, on the cusp of Christmas Day, the Doctor waited for a sign of recovery from the TARDIS. While he floated high above Earth, the people on the planet below celebrated; he stood in silence, thinking of all the friends he'd left behind in the past. Friends who might still be down there, surrounded by loved ones.

He patted the console affectionately.

'Just you and me for now, old girl,' he whispered. 'Just you and me.'

Being trapped in a time loop soon makes you aware of just how slowly time can pass. Every single second becomes the longest of your existence, each *tick* dragging painfully to the next *tock*.

A few hours had passed since the TARDIS stalled – the

Doctor knew this because he'd counted every second. All twelve thousand, four hundred and eleven of them.

Twelve thousand, four hundred and twelve . . . Twelve thousand, four hundred and thirteen . . .

'Enough!' the Doctor told himself, rising from his armchair. He'd been sitting for too long, with one eye on the console and the other on a dog-eared first edition of *Hercule Poirot's Christmas*.

He snapped the book shut and paced around the room.

Something *had* to change, and soon. Time War or no Time War, he couldn't stay trapped inside the TARDIS for the rest of eternity!

He strode back to the central console to analyse the chronometer again. Still it maintained that they were held in temporal orbit, trapped repeating the final second of December Twenty-fourth.

'WHY CAN'T IT JUST BE CHRISTMAS DAY?' roared the Doctor, throwing his hands into the air. And then, to his own surprise, he started laughing.

Was this what it felt like to be a child, waiting for Christmas? Was it always this *frustrating*? He longed for it to be the next day – Christmas Eve was so full of promise, but it wasn't the same as Christmas Day.

Was it *really* not midnight yet?

The Doctor checked his pocket watch.

Twelve thousand, seven hundred and seventy-seven seconds.

He sighed, slumping over the console again with his head in his hands.

Knock, knock, knock, knock!

The Doctor looked up from the console. Did he imagine that?

He glanced about the vast and empty room.

'Hello?' he called out.

Knock, knock, knock, knock!

'Definitely not imagining things, then,' the Doctor told himself, marching over to the TARDIS's wooden doors. Obediently, they swung open, exposing the mysterious, darkened void between the inner and outer dimensions of the TARDIS.

He popped his head across the threshold.

'Hello?' he called again, more loudly this time. 'Is somebody out there?'

He waited a moment.

'Anybody?'

Still no reply. *Intriguing.*

He paused, drumming his fingers on the doorframe. 'Well, sorry we missed each other! Another time, perhaps!'

With a sigh, the Doctor moved back inside, closing the TARDIS doors behind him. No point in keeping them open and letting a draught in. Although, now that he thought about it, there did seem to be a distinct chill in the air. The hairs on the back of his neck were standing on end. His breath had even begun to cloud the air in front of him.

The Doctor pulled his coat a little tighter, flicking up the collar. *Probably just a breeze from the vacuum of space,* he thought. *That must be it.* One could always find a rational explanation for things if one knew where to look.

Then he spotted something that defied rationality. There, propped against the console's central column, was a solitary envelope.

The Doctor walked slowly towards the curious item and picked it up.

It is real, then, he thought. *Not some sort of projection . . .*

He turned the envelope over in his hands, looking for clues. His name had been printed on the front, but otherwise it carried not so much as a postmark.

He tore it open.

Inside, there was a Christmas card. The front depicted a traditional Victorian street scene, the ground and buildings caked in snow – but, strangely, it was blank inside, save for the pre-printed greeting 'Happy Christmas'.

The Doctor studied the room. There was definitely nobody else with him, that much was certain . . . which meant that a plain paper envelope had somehow managed to arrive inside the TARDIS of its own accord.

He laughed at the absurdity of it.

Two laughs in one day? It felt like months since he'd so much as cracked a smile. As he stashed the envelope roughly into his pocket, he sighed. He really did miss having someone to laugh with. A friend with whom he could share the universe.

A voice suddenly sounded behind him: an eerie, ethereal chuckle that echoed ominously around the chamber.

The Doctor froze.

'I know there's someone here,' he announced, though even in the dim and dusty candlelight he could see there was no one else in the room. No one corporeal, anyway.

A ghost? he mused. *Ridiculous! A temporal phantom, perhaps?*

The Doctor wasn't entirely sure if a temporal phantom was a real thing or if he'd made up the name there and then. Still, it sounded like the sort of entity he'd deal with.

The laugh came again – *behind* him now and much closer than before. He could feel cool, moist breath on the back of his neck, prompting a shiver along his spine.

He spun round to confront the intruder . . . but again

there was no one there, and the laughing ceased immediately.

Was he going mad? It was more than possible. He'd been on his own for far too long, chasing the future while fleeing the past, talking to himself in darkened rooms.

'Best not rule it out,' he muttered to himself. In fact, he had plenty of evidence to suggest that this apparition was a result of his own insanity rather than an actual phantom – or whatever the intruder might be.

A pair of doors on the other side of the room made a groaning noise. The Doctor glanced up with a mixture of dread and curiosity, watching as they slowly swung open towards him, as though inviting him deep within the TARDIS.

'You want me to follow? Is that it?' he called out, a small smile playing on his lips as he began to walk across the room. 'Fine. But, I'm warning you, I know this TARDIS better than anyone.'

As the Doctor entered the corridor, the doors closed softly behind him and another set opened ahead, coaxing him forward on a path that led ever deeper into the TARDIS.

The section of the TARDIS that he was wandering into now was significantly less welcoming than the comfortable console room, with its rich wood panelling, bookcases and furniture. Here, the walls were formed from dull grey stone, and the floor was lost beneath a layer of dust and gravel.

Ancient, dripping candles lined his way, a row on either side casting everything in an amber haze. The Doctor found the light comforting. There was something curious about the quality of candlelight that always put him in mind of the daylight back on Gallifrey.

He could picture it now: the lush red plains, orange suns and crimson snow-capped mountains. There was a heavy scent of petrichor in this part of the TARDIS, which reminded the Doctor of the damp, chilly cloisters that lay under the Time Lords' Capitol. He took a deep breath, losing himself in the memory. Was he actually feeling homesick for Gallifrey after all these years of wandering?

He spotted an elaborate, swirling pattern in the stonework above him: the Seal of Rassilon. There were many of these seals throughout the TARDIS, the same pattern adorning almost every door and arch – perhaps even in every room. The Doctor had included it as a reminder of his heritage, of what he'd always run away from.

Or, perhaps, where I'm running to . . .

He dismissed the thought, and carried on along the corridor, the orange candlelight flickering around him as he passed rooms he hadn't ventured into in centuries. Some of these rooms had been kept by his companions, and he found himself running through their names like a roll call, under his breath. Sometimes the Doctor wondered what became of his companions after they left him – whether they did good, if they were happy . . . Occasionally, he found out the answer. Rarely, he might even go looking for it. But always – whatever happened, however they parted – they remained with the Doctor in spirit.

'Ghosts of Christmas past,' he whispered softly. 'I think I can live with that.'

He paused in front of one of the doors, his hand hovering just above its handle.

It would only take a moment to open it, he thought.

It would be so easy. One twist, and he could step into the past, remind himself of the good times.

No. That wasn't him. He'd never entered any of their rooms – not once, from the moment they left him – and he certainly wasn't about to start now.

Enough nostalgia. It was time to move on.

The Doctor turned and began to walk quickly back towards the console room. As he went, he heard one of the doors creak open behind him, but he didn't stop to check.

No going back, he told himself.

❄

Back in the console room, there was little doubt left in the Doctor's mind that something was in the TARDIS with him. First, it had left the envelope, then it had led him through the corridors. Now, it had left another surprise for him, back where he had started.

Nothing in the console room had been moved or stolen. Rather, it had been . . . *redecorated.*

The entire space was now awash with light and colour. The scanner in the ceiling had been opened, allowing a brilliant twilight glow to bleed around the room, infecting everything with a dazzling, wintry hue. Specks of dust sparkled in the air, drifting gently down around him and whirling through the room like some makeshift blizzard.

The Doctor shivered involuntarily. He could just see the console through the shining snowflake-like specks. Its panels were blinking excitedly, flashing with colour – reds, greens, yellows, blues – and its controls seemed to chirrup with life.

Tentatively, the Doctor approached. The entire console room had become strangely bewitching, which made him cautious. It was like a magical Christmas grotto, drawing him closer, and a rational explanation was proving elusive.

Beneath the console sat a small square box wrapped in deep-blue paper. A sequence of interlocking alien swirls twisted together on its surface to form a pattern emblazoned in silver ink. The Doctor recognised the pattern immediately: his name, written in Old High Gallifreyan.

'For me?' he asked, gingerly retrieving it from the floor. He held it next to his ear and shook it delicately. Nothing seemed to rattle inside, and it was altogether lighter than he'd expected.

Could it be empty? Is this a trap?

He shook it a little more violently before deciding it was probably neither. Whoever or whatever was doing all this, it had gone to a lot of effort, and the light show dazzling around him seemed far more like a gift than a threat.

What could it be?

Traditionally, of course, the Doctor knew that presents should only be opened on Christmas morning, and not before. However, as it appeared that he was destined to remain trapped in the last moment of Christmas Eve for all eternity, he threw caution to the wind and opened it anyway.

What confronted him under the paper was a simple, glowing cube, small enough to fit quite neatly in the palm of his hand. It pulsed with brilliant white light and seemed to weigh almost nothing. The Doctor could hear it whispering to him.

'What have we here?' the Doctor whispered back, beaming.

It was a Time Lord hypercube – an object used to transmit messages across the gulfs of space and time. With these hypercubes, Time Lords could package their thoughts telepathically, housing them in the tesseract and allowing the time winds to convey them to their recipients. In short, a psychic, intergalactic form of mail. All the Doctor needed to do was concentrate to make contact with it and –

Grandfather?

The Doctor's hearts skipped a beat when he heard the voice.

A figure had appeared on the opposite side of the console, its image distorted by the glass of the central column. It was a young woman, struggling to manifest through a fog of monochrome static, and yet the Doctor recognised her instantly.

'Susan?' The name caught at the back of his throat.

I don't know if you'll ever get this message, Grandfather.

The voice transported the Doctor back immediately to when they'd travelled the universe together.

He'd not seen Susan like this since he'd left her on Earth. He'd seen her, of course – but never this young again, not how he always remembered her.

It's been several years since we last saw one another . . . I like to think you're still out there, watching over us. Maybe that you even visit

Earth every once in a while.

The vision of Susan hesitated.

I miss you, Grandfather. And I know you must miss me. But I wanted to send this message because . . . because you were right. About me starting a new life, a life of my own.

I've been setting down roots with David. We've a child now. We called him Alex. I thought you ought to know. You're a great-grandfather, Grandfather!

She laughed excitedly, and the Doctor smiled sadly.

It's Christmas in a few weeks. Our first proper one with Alex. Earth is like another world at Christmas! I didn't realise humans had so many different traditions. I don't think I'll ever fully understand all of them – but it feels right that we should celebrate together. As a family.

That's why I'm sending this message, I suppose. Not just to let you know about Alex. But to remind you, wherever you are, that you're always more than welcome here. I know Alex and David would love to see you. I'd love to see you. And, if you could see what the humans have accomplished since the Daleks invaded, I think you'd be proud.

The Doctor nodded. More than proud. Of course he was.

Give my love to Ian and Barbara, won't you?

She paused as her voice faltered slightly.

Goodbye, Grandfather.

'Goodbye, my dear,' the Doctor said softly.

And, with that, the image evaporated into the ether, lost forever more.

The Doctor closed his eyes. That message must have taken centuries to reach him, and yet it couldn't have come at a better time. Susan had given him so much hope in those few short moments – especially in the face of things to come. If Earth had survived the Daleks, so could Gallifrey. And if Susan had started a new life, so could he.

The Time War didn't have to be the end.

When the Doctor opened his eyes, he was surprised to discover that the festive mirage had vanished. Instead, the console room was just as it had always been. No flashing lights, no blizzard – just a magnificent time and space machine.

He ran his fingers lightly across the console.

'Did *you* do all this?' he wondered, smiling softly.

It was the sort of thing the TARDIS would do. The pair of them were linked telepathically, after all. They had been since the day they fled Gallifrey. Just as he knew when the TARDIS was hurting, so it did him.

As if to answer his question, the TARDIS lurched alarmingly, throwing him off his feet. The Cloister Bell rolled, the console room trembled, then almost instantly the

TARDIS righted itself once more.

'I'll take that as a yes!' the Doctor cried.

He picked himself up off the floor and studied the read-outs. 'Hold on – that can't be! Did you just . . .?'

The TARDIS whirred approvingly, its background hum rising, just for a second.

The Doctor laughed. 'You cheeky thing!'

It was Christmas Day. The TARDIS had broken free from the time loop. Though, come to think of it, the Doctor was no longer sure if it had even been trapped there at all. Perhaps the TARDIS had simply chosen not to move. Maybe it had wanted to give him time – and what better time to give someone than Christmas?

Christmas, the Doctor realised, *forces you to remember, the good times as well as bad.*

It was a time for family, wherever and whenever they might be.

It wasn't a time for giving up, but rather a time for hope.

'Onwards!' The Doctor leaped to action, and dashed breathlessly round the console, as the TARDIS began to slowly dematerialise.

THE RED BICYCLE

Written by Gary Russell

Illustrated by Rohan Eason

There was no denying it: it was a depressing building. And the Doctor had known some depressing buildings in his time. The Lament School of Toriss, the Great Tower of Lower Mudlun, the Undercity Sewer Temple in Megropolis Six . . . it was a long list of dank, dreary places that all seemed to celebrate misery.

So, as the Doctor regarded the Powell Estate in South East London on a winter's day in 1998, his admiration for Jackie Tyler grew. (Mind you, his admiration for her was pretty much non-existent up to this point, so a rise of any kind was a sort of victory.) To bring up Rose here was a feat the Doctor had not previously appreciated; it must have taken an iron will and sheer guts, not to mention a fair bit of compromise, without Rose's dad, Pete Tyler, around to help. Oh, the Doctor knew there'd been Billys and Jims, and even a sailor called Sharkey, to keep the widow Tyler company, but none of them had helped to shape Rose into the brilliant young lady she was now. That was all thanks to Jackie.

The Doctor's thoughts were interrupted by a kid on a bike speeding by, splashing the browny-white slush that covered the street all over the Doctor's trousers. A murky puddle formed around his boots.

'Thank you!' the Doctor yelled sarcastically. He got a non-verbal response in the form of a hand gesture that he didn't understand, but wasn't entirely convinced was polite.

'Don't know why I bother sometimes,' he muttered, rubbing his ears against the biting wind that was whipping round the concrete corners of the housing estate.

The door to the stairwell that went up the side of the block where Rose and Jackie lived flew open, and a momentary glare of sulphurous light escaped into the gloom. The Doctor saw his targets emerge.

Jackie Tyler and twelve-year-old Rose were off to see Nanna Prentice for Christmas Eve. The Doctor knew he had only an hour or so to get into their flat, leave the surprise under the tree (assuming they *had* a tree) and get out again.

He felt for the sonic screwdriver in his pocket. *Useless on deadlocks*, he thought, *but on normal rim locks – piece of cake!*

This whole scheme had started a few weeks back. They were in the TARDIS, and the Doctor was explaining to Rose 'the Laws of Time and how not to break them in three easy lessons'. She had wanted to know what levels of time law-breaking were acceptable; the Doctor had told her 'none', but she had claimed that this seemed unlikely, since every time they went anywhere or did anything they changed time for someone. So the Doctor had tried to explain that, no matter where they went, they did what they did because time was *meant* to work that way.

Rose had left it at that. But a few days later, while on a visit to Earth in 1977, she had nipped out to a record shop in Piccadilly Circus and bought an album by The Stranglers that she knew Grandad Prentice had forbidden her mum from owning. Rose had then sneaked into young Jackie's bedroom and – briefly horrified by her mum's fashion choices – placed the album among the David Essex and Showaddywaddy LPs.

After that, the next time the Doctor and Rose had visited Jackie, Rose had brought up this particular album. Sure enough, her mum announced that she'd had a copy for years. She went and dug it out, saying Colin Bennett must have loaned it to her at school and she'd never given it back.

Later, back in the TARDIS, Rose had said, with a triumphant twinkle in her eye, 'See! Time didn't fall apart just because we changed one fragment of my mum's life.'

'I'm just glad that enjoying The Stranglers didn't make Jackie date this Colin person, never meet Pete Tyler and thus wipe *you* from existence!'

'Maybe I was always *meant* to do what I did,' Rose argued. 'Life is full of risks, Doctor. If you don't take them, why bother living?'

He sighed, opting to simply let it go.

Except that he *hadn't* let it go.

In fact, it had got him thinking. Remembering what one of his old tutors at the Prydon Academy on Gallifrey had said about 'causal realities' (in other words, why *not* to do exactly what Rose had just done), he started to question his assumptions. After all, he had no empirical evidence – just what one crumbly old schoolteacher had told him was the way things were. The Doctor now realised that, in all the years he had spent running away from Gallifrey, he had never actually put that teacher's claims to the test.

It is a risk, the Doctor thought. *But Rose is right. Sometimes risks have to be taken.*

A few days later, in a casual conversation at the Zaggit

'There was a big red flash. I thought it was a Christmas light
exploding or something. Then this big, big guy – tall as a house –
was there, yelling about sniffing out his doctor.
Then he nicked your bike.'

The Red Bicycle

Written by Gary Russell

Illustrated by Rohan Eason

As he thrashed and writhed in the grip of the red lightning,
a voice boomed from the glowing speaker.
'It is useless to resist, Doctor!'

Loose Wire

Written by Richard Dungworth

Illustrated by Captain Kris

Maisie smiled. This is a once-in-a-lifetime opportunity, *she reminded herself. Another once-in-a-lifetime opportunity, if such a thing were possible.*

The Gift

Written by Scott Handcock

Illustrated by Ashling Lindsay

The water was definitely moving, a short distance from where they stood. Waves appeared, small at first, then larger and larger.

The Persistence of Memory

Written by Colin Brake

Illustrated by Tom Duxbury

Zagoo bar on Zog, Rose had mentioned that when she was twelve she had begged Jackie to buy her a red bike that she had seen at the local Hildreth's. As an adult, Rose realised that Jackie could never have afforded it, but at the time she had a massive falling-out with her mum, and for a good six months afterwards resented Jackie. A lot of pre-teen angst and moodiness had begun because of the absence of that red bike.

Leaving Rose chatting to a couple of friendly Habrians, the Doctor had scooted off.

He was a Time Lord on a mission!

So now here he was: on Rose's thirteenth Christmas Eve, outside her home, with the exact red bike from Hildreth's. He'd bought it with real Earth money, and had even wrapped it in sparkly Christmas paper with Father Christmas, reindeer and glitter on it. He was rather proud of his handiwork.

Twelve-year-old Rose was going to love it! And, assuming the universe and the entire Web of Time didn't crash about his ears, he was looking forward to revealing to her one day in the future exactly what he'd done.

Jackie and Rose were out of sight. *Time for action.*

He turned to grab the bike, which was behind him.

Wrapped in sparkly paper.

With reindeer and Father Christmas and glitter on it.

Festive paper that was now lying forlornly in a puddle of slush . . . while of the bike – Rose's special red bike – there was no sign.

Panicked, the Doctor was already inputting a code on the sonic, homing in on the bike.

I've touched it enough that my DNA will be easily trackable, he thought.

'Oh, come on!' the Doctor cried in dismay as the sonic showed over eight thousand Doctor-DNA registers in London alone. He'd spent a lot of his nine lives having adventures in London.

He looked down at the soggy wrapping paper, then spotted the sticky tape.

If I can input the chemical make-up of that tape, he figured, *and add my DNA to it, the sonic should zero in on any strands of tape still attached to the bike!*

He gave it a go . . . and was pleased to see it worked.

Fantastic!

The sonic revealed that the bike was moving at a slow but constant speed. The Doctor turned on the spot, sonic outstretched.

About ninety metres in . . . that direction!

And the Doctor was off, running after whoever it was who had stolen Rose's red bike.

He dashed through the streets of Camberwell, close to the park. Then across the main road and down a side street, towards the playground next to the church where Jackie and Pete Tyler had got married. Then left, towards a small underpass where the lights never worked. The Doctor held his sonic aloft as he ran through the underpass, re-energising all the lights for the next twenty years – and probably stopping a number of muggings, graffiti murals and surreptitious snogging meet-ups that would have otherwise taken place there. More tiny changes to the timeline, no doubt – but, provided he didn't wake up tomorrow and find humanity had been replaced by apes or sophisticated dinosaurs, he was OK with that.

There! The Doctor spotted a young lad in a snorkel parka and red baseball cap on a bike – and pedalling furiously, now that he realised he was being chased.

Gotcha! the Doctor thought.

At which point a black cab zoomed past, showering him for a second time that day in sludge and sleet. By the time the taxi had passed, the boy on the stolen bike was nowhere to be seen. The Doctor looked left and right, then stared down at his sonic. No trace.

That was weird, he thought. *He was here only a moment ago.*

The Doctor glanced around – he was just at the foot of Denmark Hill, close to the Hildreth's where he had bought Rose's bike.

Maybe I should just get another one? he wondered.

Moments later, he was peering through the window of the darkened shop. *Of course, bike shops tend not to be open at 7.30 p.m. on Christmas Eve,* he thought grumpily.

And, anyway, as far as he could see there were no other red bikes on display.

The Doctor toyed with the idea of using the TARDIS to travel back a few minutes so he could stop the thief, then leave the bike somewhere his five-minute-earlier self could find it.

But then BANG! *goes the Web of Time again,* he thought. *And a possible Blinovitch limitation effect if two Doctors come into contact with one another. The bike itself could accidentally get imbued with their identical artron energy and* BANG! *There goes planet Earth, half of Mutter's Spiral and a time quake through history, back and forth. No,* he decided. *Best to just find the bike. That will be safer all round.*

He was suddenly aware of a young lad standing beside him, also staring in at the bikes. Red baseball cap, snorkel parka, shaking slightly.

The bike thief!

The Doctor's initial annoyance at what the boy had done

was replaced by concern; this lad was clearly in shock.

'Are you OK?' the Doctor asked, already knowing that the lad wasn't.

The boy shook his head. He looked at the Doctor. 'Sorry about the bike. Was it your kid's?'

'A Christmas present for a friend,' the Doctor said. 'And you really shouldn't have nicked it.'

'Sorry. Won't happen again.'

'Good to know,' the Doctor said. 'But, more importantly, what happened to it?'

'I dunno. There was a big red flash. I thought it was a Christmas light exploding or something. Then this big, big guy – tall as a house – was there, yelling about sniffing out his doctor. Then he nicked your bike.'

'Which you nicked in the first place.'

'Splitting hairs,' the boy said, his bravado coming back.

'What happened then?'

'Another red light and he was gone.' The boy started to walk away, clearly done with the Doctor now. 'Oh, and he was made of metal,' he added, looking over his shoulder.

The Doctor considered this. He had a lot of enemies, and Christmas was not really something that encouraged them to stop hunting him.

'Hey, you,' he called after the departing boy. 'Where was

this big metal guy with the red light?'

The boy looked back one last time, then pointed up Denmark Hill. 'Up by the train station, mate.' Then he was gone, swallowed up by the dark and the slight Christmas drizzle that was kicking off.

Checking his sonic, the Doctor trudged up the hill and turned left towards the railway station. After a few moments he stopped and sniffed. The air was crisp, different here. Just in one small place. A circle about the size of a car where there was no snow or sludge. He ran his finger along the now very defined edge of the white ground and sniffed it. *Ozone.*

He tweaked his sonic to detect ozone, gave it a quick blast, then hurried back to the TARDIS.

Back inside the ship, the Doctor shoved the sonic into a special slot that he called the Sonic's Detector Slot. As he'd once told Rose, the sonic detected things while in that slot. It wasn't a very imaginative name.

Right now, the sonic was tracing that very distinct ozone signature back to wherever it had come from.

With a *ping* and a *bong*, the TARDIS landed and the Doctor stepped outside.

'Oh.' He sighed, immediately unimpressed, but also on high alert.

The big sign in front of him told him exactly where he was: Jinko's Scrap And Junk. Best Grotzits Paid.

He was in the Andromeda Galaxy. Not really somewhere he wanted to be. The last time he had been here, the aforementioned Jinko had made it very clear that he did not want to see the Doctor ever again. The Doctor had no desire to see Jinko again either, and yet here he was.

Jinko was an eighteen-foot-tall lifeform made entirely out of customised junk metal. He rebuilt himself periodically, when something new came into his scrapyard that could house his colossal brain. With the right upbringing, Jinko could have been an amazing politician, or a brilliant writer, or a genius inventor, or a scholar; instead, he was a scrap merchant doing dodgy deals for shonky wrecked flyers and speeders and appliances, which he then cut up in his chop-shop and sold on in equally dodgy deals.

He'd actually sold a friend of the Doctor a 'rather brilliant new planetary hopper'. The price paid should have been a warning (it was cheap as chips), but the Doctor's friend was bedazzled by the shiny vehicle and forgot to be sensible. The hopper literally disintegrated as it hit the atmosphere of Carolian IV; the Doctor's friend was only saved by the Doctor materialising the TARDIS around him.

The Doctor's chum was more than a little displeased, shouting about how Jinko needed to get what was coming to him. However, given that he was a three-foot-tall Zocci with a pork-pie hat and a monocle, the Doctor suspected any confrontation would be likely to go Jinko's way. So he had deposited his friend safely home, before returning to confront Jinko himself.

Jinko, unsurprisingly, refused to return the grotzits he'd received for the hopper, and an angry argument ensued, in which the Doctor had used his sonic to reduce much of Jinko's illegal 'merchandise' to molten metal. As the Doctor made his escape, he had clearly heard Jinko swearing vengeance and announcing that one day he'd melt the TARDIS down to its liquefied origins, preferably with the Time Lord still inside.

That had been about a hundred years ago, relatively speaking, so Jinko was a cyborg with a long-held grudge.

And, now, a red bike that did not belong to him.

Taking a deep breath, the Doctor walked into the scrapyard, which had been refilled with numerous metallic machines, none of which looked legitimate or entirely spaceworthy. Every junk pile was laid out a bit like an interconnected maze, so that customers – most of whom were probably as crooked and deceitful as Jinko – could walk between huge walls of scrap to find whatever junk they needed.

That was the Andromeda Galaxy for you: a hideout for rogues, thieves and other unsavoury characters. Sometimes the Doctor felt right at home here; other times, less so. It depended on what body he was wearing at the time.

Right now, the Doctor felt rather confident. Jinko hadn't seen him in this new, tough exterior, and the freshly cropped hair and leather jacket would present a more formidable presence than the last time he had been here, in a long green velvet coat, grey cravat and Byronesque hairdo. That look had proven to be somewhat of a disadvantage in Jinko's scrapyard.

'Hey, Jinko!' the Doctor yelled into the gloom. 'Where's my red bike?'

There was no answer, but three menacing figures suddenly stepped out of the darkness. Each one was dressed in a spiked leather jacket and swinging a hefty-looking ball and chain. They weren't human. They were Elians – hired muscle with little brain but a great deal of stamina.

Trust Jinko to surround himself with Elians, the Doctor thought.

The Doctor didn't have a clue how he was going to get out of this. Jinko, at least, could communicate with words – even if they didn't have too many syllables – but Elians tended to know 'uggh', 'urrkk' and 'die', and not much else.

'Oh, c'mon, Jinko. It's me. You know I don't talk to the
hired help. I'm the Doctor! I watched the Andromedans
invade the Hagon Cluster and sent them scurrying back here,
tails between their legs, with my words. You think these thugs
scare me?'

This was a slight exaggeration, but Jinko was unlikely to
know that.

The Elians started to move slowly towards the Doctor,
swinging their weapons threateningly.

Oh, this is not going to go as it should, is it? the Doctor thought
unhappily.

He quickly scanned the mountains of metal junk around
him, and there he spotted a solution. 'Brilliant!' he whispered.

He whipped the sonic out and aimed it at a teetering pile
of metal to his left, then sent out a pulse and nimbly stepped
to the side.

This made two of the Elians step forward. They
immediately found themselves encased in a huge, hollow
metal tube that crashed down from where the Doctor's sonic
had vibrated it loose. The sheer force of the fall buried it
several centimetres into the ground. The Elians were trapped.

'Two down. One more to go!' the Doctor said to himself.

Annoyingly, the third Elian had been fractionally cleverer
– maybe suspecting a trap – and hadn't moved. He was now

waving his massive chain round his head like a bola, and strode forward.

The Doctor glanced around. Elians were stupid, but not that stupid. The Doctor wouldn't be able to pull off the same trick twice.

As the chain spun towards him, the Doctor jumped on to what seemed to be the hood of a rusty old land-speeder. The chain crashed down beside him, gouging a huge rent in the metal with a clang that made his ears ring. He clambered forward, scrabbling into the junk pile. The Elian's chain struck again, just clipping the back of his Dr. Martens – not enough to damage them, but enough to knock him off balance. He fell to the ground and looked up . . . and saw that the entire pile of junk was going to crash down on him.

He rolled away as fast as he could, and only just avoided the destruction the junk wrought as it thundered to the ground.

He sat up and looked around. Either the Elian had been crushed to death under all the junk – which was not what the Doctor had intended – or he was trapped on the other side. The crashing sound of the chain confirmed the latter.

The Doctor scurried backwards to safety.

Maybe Rose's bike is not really worth upsetting Jinko over, he considered. But, in his mind's eye, he could see twelve-year-old Rose on Christmas morning, ripping the wrapping paper away and revealing her beautiful new red bicycle, while a very surprised but smart-enough-to-just-take-the-credit Jackie sat next to her. The Doctor was determined to get the bike back.

Suddenly Jinko was towering above him, dangling Rose's bike from his massive metal hand.

'Is this what you came for, Doctor?' Jinko boomed.

'Well, to be honest,' the Doctor replied, 'you sort of came for it first. I just followed your less-than-well-hidden trail.'

'I wanted you to find me,' Jinko snapped back.

'I figured. Otherwise why nick the bike?'

'I have been sniffing out your DNA for years now.'

'Not literally, I assume, seeing as you don't have a nose – or any internal organs capable of detecting anything.'

'I have machines!' roared the giant scrap merchant angrily. 'They were programmed to find you.'

'And so they did,' the Doctor said. 'Which is very nice and lovely –' he got to his feet – 'but right now, if it's OK with you, I'd like my friend's bike back.'

'No. You will suffer for the insult you paid me!' Jinko roared.

'I've insulted lots of people,' the Doctor replied. 'I'm really very good at it. It's almost a career actually. And, anyway, what makes my insulting you worth all this bother? It must have taken *ages* to build all those DNA-hunting devices to track me down, and then the best you can do is nick my bike? I mean, you don't take the TARDIS, or my sonic –' to underscore this, the Doctor tossed the sonic in his hand. 'No. You nick a silly little Earth bicycle. Bit sad, eh?'

Furious, Jinko let go of the bike.

The Doctor leaped forward and caught the bike in mid-air, getting winded in the process.

'One thing about you, Jinko,' the Doctor said, catching his breath. 'You're very predictable. You build your scrapyards like you build yourself – very unimaginatively. So, if I were to do this –' the Doctor aimed his sonic at the wall of junk behind Jinko – 'and this –' he fired the sonic – 'I reckon, rather like dominoes, the whole lot would come crashing down.'

He was quite right.

With a noise unlike anything the Doctor had heard before, Jinko disappeared from sight behind a wall of falling metal.

Unfortunately, all the other mountains of junk began to topple as well, threatening to flatten the Doctor like a pancake.

He jumped on the red bike and pedalled as fast as he could towards the TARDIS, swerving round falling metal objects on his way – no easy task on a kid's bike.

For a brief moment, that third Elian stood in front of the TARDIS doors, then he was swept aside by a metal girder that was swinging back and forth.

That was lucky! the Doctor thought as he ducked under the girder and whizzed straight through the TARDIS doors.

Jumping off the bike, he slammed the doors shut and rammed the TARDIS into dematerialisation mode.

With a smile, he patted the bike. 'Merry Christmas, Rose Tyler.'

Twelve-year-old Rose looked at the label on the bike: To MY FAVOURITE ROSE. LOVE FROM FATHER CHRISTMAS.

Rose looked at Jackie. 'Awww, thanks, Mum!' She gave Jackie a hug – the first that Jackie had had from her daughter in a long while.

As Rose dashed outside to test her new bike on the street below, Jackie stood by the front door, looking around as though trying to see who had really left the bike. But there was no one, and no clue . . . besides an odd square indentation in the slushy snow.

It was as if something had recently been there, but was now long gone.

LOOSE WIRE

Written by Richard Dungworth

Illustrated by Captain Kris

Alice Wu's Christmases had all come at once. For starters, her parents had got her exactly what she had been hoping for: her very own smartphone. Compared to her old phone, which didn't even have a touchscreen, the new one was *seriously* cool.

Her grandmother, too, had done an excellent job. Over the last few weeks, Gran had dropped several hints that she was knitting Alice 'a nice, sensible cardigan'. This, to Alice's great relief, had turned out to be a deliberate wind-up. In reality, Gran had given her a gorgeous pair of earrings and next year's Justin Bieber calendar – both high on Alice's wish list.

Then there were the sprouts. Somehow they had

dropped off Mum's online supermarket order. As far as Alice was concerned, a sprout-free Christmas dinner was a major result.

And now, with the delicious meal over, her big brother had just declared that – since Christmas afternoon was 'always pretty lame' at their house – he was going to spend it at his girlfriend's. For Alice, his departure was yet another reason to be cheerful. Now there was a good chance that she'd get to choose which movie they would watch together later on the brand-new smart TV her father had bought 'for Mum'.

For now, though, the grown-ups had control of the remote. Mum, Dad and Gran had all settled themselves in the front room to watch the queen deliver her annual Christmas message. Alice had taken the chance to slip upstairs to her bedroom with her new phone. Now that its battery was charged, she was keen to see what it could do. She decided to try a video call to her best friend, Tasha, first.

Perched on her bed, she peeled away the transparent film protecting the new phone's screen (why *was* that *so* satisfying?). She extracted the little SIM card from her old phone and, after a quick look at the instruction leaflet, slotted it into the new one. All set. She pressed the phone's power button and waited for it to boot up.

To her surprise, the phone immediately began to ring.

Its inbuilt video-messaging app popped-up to fill the screen. Alice read the caller ID below the green pick-up button.

Unknown caller.

Alice knew all about the dangers of phone pests, and usually ignored anonymous calls. But she had a hunch this one might be Tasha. Her friend had been holding out for a new phone too. If she had a new number, Alice's phone wouldn't have recognised it.

Alice pressed the pick-up button. The phone's screen filled with a young man's smiling face – and Alice's heart missed a beat.

The caller wasn't unknown at all. He was world famous. Alice recognised him instantly. The styled hair, the hazel eyes, the perfect teeth and flawless skin . . .

Her eyes shot to the calendar already in pride of place on her bedroom wall, then back to the phone screen.

'Justin?' she said feebly.

'Hey, Alice.'

The familiar soft Canadian drawl gave Alice goosebumps. She gaped at her phone in disbelief.

'Alice, listen. I'm counting on you to help me out.'

Alice somehow found her voice.

'*You* want *my* help?'

'Uh-huh. I need to get my mojo back. Feel re-energised.'

'I . . . I don't understand.'

There was something not quite right about the golden-brown eyes. Alice thought she could see threads of red light dancing across their whites. She tried to break their hold – and found she couldn't.

'I'm hungry, Alice.'

The fizzling lines of crimson were growing clearer, brighter, spreading.

'D-do you want me to . . . order you some food . . . or something?' murmured Alice, mesmerised.

'*I'm hunnnggrryyyy!*'

The phone's screen began to glow with blood-red energy. For some reason, Alice felt compelled to touch it. She was just reaching out with one forefinger –

When a man in a pinstriped suit and baseball sneakers exploded through her bedroom door.

'DROP IT!'

The man's shout broke Alice's trance. She turned to look at him in surprise – and his dark brown eyes blazed back at her, full of fierce intent. He was brandishing a slim silver device, not unlike a torch, as though it were a firearm.

'Step away from the phone!' he commanded.

As Alice sat frozen, dumbstruck, another voice filled the room with a wild cry of rage.

'YOU!'

The hate-filled howl had come from Alice's new phone. She saw, to her horror, that the face on its screen had undergone a monstrous transformation. It was contorted in a grotesque, inhuman snarl and bathed in blood-red light. Its livid eyes were glaring at the stranger. The entire phone was crackling with red energy.

With great effort, Alice tore her eyes from it once again and threw it down on her duvet. She sprang away from the bed. As she did so, a stream of flickering red light came lashing out at her from the incandescent phone.

'Oh no you don't!'

The stranger in the suit leaped forward, jabbing out his handheld device. Its glowing tip intercepted the path of the crimson lightning.

There was a dazzling explosion of light. As Alice screwed her eyes up against the glare, she heard another roar of fury. It was abruptly silenced by an ear-splitting crack.

Then . . . peace.

Heart thumping, Alice opened her eyes.

The stranger was prodding warily at something at the foot of her bed. Something smouldering and sparking, its metallic skin charred and black. He tried to pick it up, then dropped it with a yelp.

'Ow-ow! Hot-hot-hot!' Blowing on his fingers, he looked at Alice. 'You OK?'

Alice stared back at him, then at the smoking thing on the floor.

'What have you done to my phone?' she wailed.

The man deflected the question with one of his own. 'Didn't anyone tell you not to talk to strangers?'

Alice felt her hackles rise. She never liked being patronised.

'It wasn't a stranger,' she said indignantly. 'It was Justin Bieber!'

'Pff!' snorted the man, with an annoyingly knowing expression. 'Don't you *belieb* it.' He chuckled to himself.

Alice's irritation was growing. Who even *was* this guy?

'*You're* a stranger,' she said, scowling at him. 'Actually, you're an intruder, which is even worse!'

'*Me?* An intruder? Don't be daft!' he scoffed. Then, after a moment, he frowned. 'Although, I suppose, *technically* . . .'

He turned his attention back to what was left of Alice's phone, attempting to pick it up again.

Alice persisted. 'Why are you in my house?' she demanded.

The man wasn't listening. He was fully absorbed in examining the stricken smartphone. It had evidently cooled

enough to handle. Perched on Alice's bed, he peered at the
phone closely, shone his odd, buzzing gadget into it, and even
sniffed at it. He looked increasingly puzzled.

'What?' he muttered, scanning the phone's scorched
screen again. '*What?!* How can it *not* be here?'

Suddenly he sprang to his feet.

'Gargh! Of course!' He slammed the heel of one palm
against his forehead once, twice, three times. 'Stupid, stupid,
stupid!'

He turned to Alice. His eyes were bright with urgency
again.

'Was this paired with anything?'

Alice gave him a puzzled look. 'How do you mean?'

'Wirelessly connected. To a speaker, maybe? Or
headphones?'

'No.'

'Anything like that in the house?' demanded the stranger.
'Anything Bluetooth-enabled?'

Alice felt another rush of annoyance. Why was *he*
asking all the questions? Hadn't he just burst into her room
unannounced and fried her new phone? For all she knew, he
was here to steal her family's possessions or something.

She gave him her best frosty look. 'Why should I tell you?'

'Because . . .' Peering past her, the man read from one

of the certificates stuck to her pinboard. 'Because, Alice Jane Wu, Grade Three with Merit –' his eyes returned to hers – 'there is a very real chance that very bad things will happen if you don't.'

'To me?' said Alice, a little unnerved. It had sounded a lot like a threat. But somehow, as she held the stranger's gaze, Alice felt instinctively that he meant her no harm. His expression was earnest, not menacing.

'To *everyone*,' he said gravely.

Alice made a gut decision. She had no idea what was going on, but for now she would give this man the benefit of the doubt.

'Max has a Bluetooth speaker,' she said. 'In his room.'

'Show me!'

Alice quickly led the way upstairs to Max's attic bedroom. The stranger raised an eyebrow as he surveyed the chaos.

'High level of entropy, musky odour . . .'

The clothing strewn on the unmade bed was mostly black. There was a poster for a grim-looking band called *Apocalypz* over the headboard.

'Nihilistic tendencies. I'm getting moody male, late teens.' He looked at Alice. 'Max is your big brother, right?'

'Uh-huh. It's kind of a lair, more than a bedroom.'

'And his speaker?'

'Buried somewhere in this lot.'

'Course it is.'

He immediately began rummaging through the mess, eyeing a pile of *Decibel* magazines with slight alarm as he searched behind them. 'Thrash metal, eh? Not my cup of tea, I'm afraid. Give me good old rock 'n' roll any day. And an actual cup of tea, of course.'

Alice joined the hunt, getting increasingly curious. A moment later the stranger gave a triumphant cry as he shifted a battered guitar case to the side.

'Aha!'

Even as he uncovered the speaker, it flared with red light. A stream of crackling crimson energy burst from its front. As the stranger raised his buzzing gadget, the red light lashed at his hand.

'Aaargh!'

His arm spasmed violently and he dropped the silver device.

More energy streams came whipping out from the speaker. As they latched on to the man's face, his neck arched back and he let out an agonised cry.

'Nyyaaaaaaaaaaaarrrrgh!'

As he thrashed and writhed in the grip of the red

lightning, a voice boomed from the glowing speaker.

'It is useless to resist, Doctor!'

There was something in its arrogant tone that Alice recognised.

'I have feasted, and I am *strong*!' it snarled. 'Yet still . . . so . . . *HUUUNNGGGRRYYYY*!'

Alice watched the effect of the red streams in horror. They were dragging at the man's face, distorting his features, blurring them, *erasing* them . . .

Alice broke out of her horrified stupor. She snatched the stranger's silver gadget from where it had fallen, then drove its still-flickering tip into the heart of the red maelstrom that swirled around the speaker.

There was another blinding flash. Another howl of rage. Another deafening crack.

Alice was thrown backwards against the side of her brother's bed.

Then, thank goodness, all was calm. Alice bathed in the silence for a few seconds, feeling her pulse slowly steady. She heard a long, low groan from nearby.

The stranger was lying on his back, slowly reviving. Alice hurried over to him and helped him sit up – and was mightily relieved to see that his face was back to normal. He was dazed, but seemed unhurt.

'Thank you, Alice Jane Wu,' he said groggily. '*That* deserved a distinction.'

The speaker threw off a last crackling spark, making Alice start. She looked at it woefully.

'Max'll kill me,' she said. 'He won't be able to play his music.'

The stranger managed a weak smile. 'The neighbours will be gutted,' he said.

He tried to get to his feet, groaned, and plonked himself down again.

'What *was* that?' pressed Alice. 'What attacked you?'

'Residual electrical essence of an executed alien criminal,' the stranger replied flatly.

'Right. I see,' said Alice, who really didn't.

'Calls itself "the Wire". It's a voracious predator. Consumes the neural energy of others. It can feed on the electrical activity of a victim's brain.'

'It looked like it was trying to suck your face off.'

'Mmm.' The stranger massaged his temples with his fingertips. 'I'd forgotten how much it burns. Gets you right behind the eyes.'

'It called you "doctor". Is that what you are? A doctor?'

'*The* Doctor. No prescribing stuff. More preventing pan-galactic catastrophe. And slightly better hours.'

The Doctor made a second attempt to get up. With
a little assistance from Alice, he managed to stand – albeit
rather unsteadily. He looked at her, frowning. 'Was it just me,
or did it sound like Simon Cowell?'

That was who it sounded like! thought Alice, and she
nodded.

The Doctor grunted. 'I guess if you're aiming for the
essence of nastiness . . .' he said. 'Anyway. Seems like it's
expanding its repertoire.'

'How do you mean?' asked Alice.

'The Wire's a mimic. It has the ability to adopt any
visual or aural identity it encounters in the form of electrical
transmission.' The Doctor bent to retrieve his gadget from
where Alice had dropped it. 'Justin Bieber. Simon Cowell.
Anyone from Kylie to the queen.'

'*Anyone?*'

Alice felt her stomach tighten. A sudden sense of
foreboding gripped her. She turned and dashed for the door.
Within seconds, she had bounded down two flights of stairs
and burst into the living room . . .

Only to have her worst fears confirmed.

'*No!*' she sobbed. 'Mum! Gran! Dad!'

The brand-new forty-inch smart TV was on. Its screen,
however, displayed only the words NO SIGNAL. Despite this,

Alice's mother and grandmother were facing it, motionless and silent on the sofa. They could not be said, however, to be *watching* the TV – for the simple reason that they had no eyes to watch with. They had no features at all. Their faces were empty, inhuman blanks.

It was the same with her father. He sat in his armchair, silent and still, his typically cheery face devoid of any features at all. The only signs of life he displayed were his upright posture and the eerie twitching of his hands. They were opening and closing, and opening and closing, in the steady rhythm of a heartbeat.

Alice's cry had brought the Doctor rushing into the room. As he took in the sight of the three faceless victims, his eyes burned with outrage. He looked at Alice and his expression softened as he hurried to comfort her.

'They'll be OK, I promise,' he said. He took her by the shoulders and looked directly into her tear-filled eyes. 'We can get them back.'

Alice looked up at him. She wanted to believe him. 'How?' she asked, her voice choked with tears.

'The Wire's greed is its weakness,' said the Doctor. 'It's so ravenous that it swallows its victims whole.'

'So?' Alice wasn't finding this particularly reassuring.

'The unique neuro-electrical identity of each individual

remains intact, even once they've been consumed,' the Doctor explained. 'You know the story of Jonah? Who lived in the whale's belly when it swallowed him?'

Alice nodded.

'It's like that. They're still alive, all of them, inside the thing. We just need to catch it, and we can set them free.'

'OK.' Alice tried to pull herself together. 'Let's do it. Let's catch this . . . thing, and get my family back.'

'Atta girl!' said the Doctor, grinning.

He let go of Alice's shoulders and approached the TV set. He looked thoughtfully at the blank screen.

'This is where it came in. Over the internet, on to the telly. Then it came for you, through the router, to your phone.'

He turned back to Alice.

'I managed to tag it when it first got loose. I've been tracking it. When my tracer led me here, I locked down the area.'

He held up his silver gadget.

'Sonic screwdriver. Right now, it's transmitting an electron shroud, twenty metres across, centred *here*.' He tapped the blue tip of the device. 'It encapsulates the entire building. No electrical signal can get in or out. Not by cable, satellite, 3G, FM – not so much as a squeak.' He smiled a sly smile. 'Which means the Wire has no way to escape.'

Alice brightened a little. 'So, it's *already* trapped?'

'Weeeell . . .' The Doctor looked awkward. '*Kind* of. You
see, I sort of forgot about short-range wireless technology,'
he admitted sheepishly. 'Bluetooth connections and the like.
It's using them to jump from one device to another within the
shroud.' He frowned. 'They're not Net-based, so my tracer's
lost the scent.'

As Alice tried to take all this in, a thought struck her.

'Dad tried Max's speaker once, when he first got it. He
paired it to his phone.' She pointed to where a black leather
phone case sat on the nearby mantelpiece.

The Doctor approached the fireplace warily, sonic
screwdriver at the ready. He lifted the case and gingerly
carried it to the coffee table, then quickly slid the phone out
on to the table's surface.

Nothing happened.

The Doctor picked up the phone. To Alice's
bewilderment, he licked its screen. He shook his head. 'Not
here. But it's been *through* here.'

He switched the phone on, and fiddled silently with it for
a few seconds. Then –

'Ah. That's not good.' The Doctor looked at Alice. 'By
which I mean it's very bad.'

Through the room's bay window, Alice heard the sudden growl of a car engine being started. The Doctor's eyes grew wide. He tossed the phone on to the sofa, hurdled over its padded arm and sprinted for the door.

'Allons-y!' he cried.

'What is it?' demanded Alice as she raced after him.

'Your dad's phone!' replied the Doctor, tearing through the hall into the front porch. 'It's paired with a device called "Car 2".' He yanked the front door open, and ducked outside. 'I'm taking a wild guess that's –'

'Mum's satnav!'

The little red three-door Fiat – Alice's mother's pride and joy – was already reversing out of the driveway. There was no one inside it. Its headlights crackled with red energy.

As the Fiat swung out into the road, the Doctor sprinted after it. He aimed his sonic screwdriver. Both the car's front doors sprang open.

'Hurrah for central locking!'

He performed an athletic sliding vault across the Fiat's bonnet and dived into the driver's seat. The car was already pulling away. Alice just managed to scramble in through the passenger door before both doors slammed shut of their own accord. An eerie voice came over the car's sound system.

'Now, Doctor, it is *you* who is trapped!'

Alice shivered. Susan, the friendly voice she had helped choose for Mum's satnav, sounded a lot more evil now.

The satnav itself was aglow with red light.

'Now it is *you* who is under *my* cont–'

The voice suddenly cut off. The Doctor had torn a chunk of plastic from the underside of the dashboard. Two severed wires dangled from the mess of electrics within.

'That'll shut you up, at least,' he said. But a moment later he gave a cry of pain and thrashed back against his headrest as red energy came lashing out from the exposed wires.

The car swung left, taking the corner at the end of Alice's road at speed.

Grimacing, the Doctor seized the wheel and strained to turn it. He slammed a foot on the brake, the clutch, the accelerator – all to no effect.

'Can't override it!' he gasped. 'It's taken over the servo electronics!'

'But why take Mum's car?' cried Alice. 'It still can't get past your shield thingy, right? It's still trapped?'

She and the Doctor were both flung sideways as the Fiat screeched round another corner, out on to the main road.

'Not for long. My screwdriver *transmits* the shroud. But it's generated by my TARDIS.'

'Your what?'

'Sort of mobile home. Parked in your back garden. Once we're more than a few kilometres away, we'll be out of its range. The shroud will fail. The Wire will be able to jump to the nearest hotspot.' The Doctor looked grim. 'It'll be loose on the Net again!'

The car swerved into the path of a van coming the other way. Terrified, Alice squeezed her eyes shut. There was an angry blare from the van's horn . . .

Then, somehow, they were past it.

'Can't you do something?' she pleaded.

'The only way to truly contain the Wire is to isolate it on an analogue medium with zero connectivity,' said the Doctor. 'Last time I trapped it on a Betamax tape.'

'Last time?'

'It went on the rampage before. On the day of the queen's coronation.'

Alice frowned. 'But that was *ages* ago. How could *you* have been there?'

The Doctor gave a pained smile. 'I'm older than I look.'

Another horn sounded as the little Fiat roared wildly through a set of red traffic lights.

'How come no one ever talks about it?' said Alice. 'Gran never said.'

'The government kept it all hush-hush. Didn't want
to taint the British image.' The Doctor's tone was bitter.
'There'll be no sweeping it under the rug *this* time. It's not
just TV viewers it can feed on now. The digital age is one big
Wire picnic. YouTube browsers, social-media users – if we let
it get loose, it'll drain enough energy to manifest in *seconds*.'

'Manifest?'

'Assume its corporeal form. The physical form that was
taken from it when it was executed by its own kind.'

'What *sort* of physical form?'

'Your guess is as good as mine. But I think we can
assume it won't be cuddly.'

The Doctor made another determined attempt to wrestle
back control of the car – to no avail.

'How did it get free?' said Alice, clinging to the door
handle as they swerved. 'From the tape thing, I mean.'

'My fault, I'm afraid,' replied the Doctor gloomily. 'I
was looking for a film I'd recorded. My favourite Christmas
movie.'

He thumped the stubborn steering wheel in frustration,
then glared at the CD slot below the crimson-glowing satnav.

'Garrrgh! If only your mum's car had a good old cassette
player!'

Alice's face lit up. 'It does!'

She yanked open the glove compartment. It was all there, thank goodness: Walkman cassette player, in-car power adaptor, output lead. She grabbed the lot and hurriedly passed it over to a suddenly revitalised Doctor.

'Mum likes all her old pop stuff best. Most of it's on cassette,' she explained. 'She got Dad to rig this up so she can play her old mixtapes.'

'Hallelujah for golden oldies!' whooped the Doctor. He set about modifying the Walkman, tearing off the power adaptor and connecting the bared wires to the unlit end of his sonic screwdriver. He jabbed the output jack into the AUX socket in the dashboard – getting a fresh shock of red energy for his troubles. Gritting his teeth, he handed the Walkman back to Alice.

'OK. On three, hit RECORD. Got it?'

Alice nodded earnestly.

'Ready? *THREE!*'

As the Doctor pointed his screwdriver into the car's cigarette lighter, Alice activated the Walkman. Its tape spoolers squealed, spinning at supercharged speed.

Alice squeezed her eyes shut against the flash of red light that filled the little car. The glare died and she heard the *pop* of the Walkman's automatic stop button. She opened her eyes, and immediately saw that the satnav was no longer ablaze.

There was a harsh chorus of horns as the car shot out on to a roundabout, now totally out of control. The Doctor seized the wheel and rammed both feet down on the brake pedal. The car careered straight on to the roundabout's central island and came to a halt, engine stalled, in a large bed of Christmas roses.

At last, the chaos ceased.

Alice looked down warily at the Walkman, now in her lap. It gave off a final sputter of red sparks and then was silent.

The Doctor leaned from the driver's seat to grab the machine. He ejected the cassette from within it, and sniffed at it eagerly. His face lit up.

'Oh, *yes*.' He beamed at Alice. 'Job's a good 'un!'

Alice felt the tension leave her body. She lay back limply in her seat.

'Mind you,' said the Doctor, examining the cassette's label with mock concern. 'I doubt your mum'll be too chuffed we've taped over *Cliff at Christmas*.'

'No more "Mistletoe and Wine",' said Alice. 'That *is* a terrible thought.' She grinned. 'So, what now?'

With a look of renewed purpose, the Doctor touched his sonic to the ignition. 'Back to the TARDIS,' he replied, as the Fiat's engine fired. 'We've got a whale to empty!'

✸

'Top up, Mr Smith?'

'Ooh! Don't mind if I do, Mrs Wu.'

The Doctor held out his teacup for Alice's mother to refill from the pot. He beamed at her from his spot on the sofa. He had a plate piled with delicious Christmas dinner on his knee.

'Thank you. Lovely cuppa.'

Alice, sitting between the Doctor and Gran, was feeling full of the festive spirit. Her family was watching TV together, comfortable and very full from dinner, in classic Christmas-afternoon style. It was hard to believe that only an hour ago three of them had been faceless, silent, twitching.

It had been quite an hour.

Alice's visit to the Doctor's TARDIS had been as memorable as her nail-biting ride in her mum's Wire-possessed car. Tasha wouldn't believe half of what Alice had to tell her.

She hadn't *fully* understood the Doctor's rapid-fire commentary as he'd taken the necessary steps to get her family back. There had been something about 'vestigial IP imprints' and 'fractionating neuro-electrical identities'. She had grasped the basic idea, though: by hooking his TARDIS's systems up with Mum's Christmas tape, the Doctor had been able to extract the electrical essence of each of the Wire's victims and transmit it to its rightful owner via the Net. The monster itself was still, thankfully, imprisoned on the cassette.

Alice wasn't bothered exactly *how* it had worked. She was just glad that it had. When she and the Doctor had hurried back into the house to find Mum, Dad and Gran laughing at an old *Two Ronnies* TV special, it had been the best gift of this or any other Christmas.

The Doctor swallowed the last of the sandwich Alice's mother had prepared for him. 'Oh, yes!' He sighed happily. 'Can't beat a nice turkey sandwich. Smidgen of cranberry sauce, bit of cold stuffing. Christmas in a mouthful!'

'You're not wrong there,' said Dad, smiling at his visitor.

Alice was amazed at how the Doctor had made himself welcome in her home so quickly. She had expected a grilling about this stranger she'd invited in, but no; the Doctor had effortlessly convinced her parents he was 'John Smith, National Grid Rapid Responder, here about the electricity surge'. His ID card, presumably fake, had sealed the deal. Even Dad had swallowed it whole. Mum and Gran had been fussing over their 'guest' ever since, horrified that 'the poor man' was not only having to work on Christmas Day, but hadn't even eaten.

The Doctor's cover had enabled him to stick around long enough to put right a couple of things that might otherwise have landed Alice in trouble. The dashboard of Mum's car was back to normal, and Max's speaker was working again – with the added feature, the Doctor had told Alice with a wink, of a 'bespoke volume limiter'.

The only casualty was Alice's frazzled smartphone. It was beyond repair, even at the Doctor's hands.

But who needs a boring smartphone? thought Alice, smiling to herself. She fished her trusty old phone from her pocket. Thanks to a little sonic-screwdriver wizardry, it was now her very own *super*phone. Its enhanced features included a direct line to her remarkable new friend in the TARDIS.

The Doctor suddenly sat forward, returning teacup to saucer. He was staring in delighted surprise at the TV.

'*No!* You're *kidding!*'

The opening sequence of a black-and-white film had just come on.

'This is it! My favourite movie! The one I was looking for when –' He gave Alice a stealthy look. 'The one I was telling you about.'

He turned back to the TV, beaming. A large, tolling bell gave way to the sound of smaller, jingling ones.

'Frank Capra's evergreen classic. It's got everything. Drama, comedy, Jimmy Stewart, angels –' he pulled a face – 'actually, I'm not mad about angels.' His smile came flashing back. 'But still, it's just *the* Christmas classic. Even the title's genius.'

Right on cue, orchestral music swelled, and the film's title appeared on the screen.

'*It's A Wonderful Life,*' Alice read aloud.

'See what I mean?' said the Doctor.

He helped himself to a mince pie from the coffee table, sat back and smiled a satisfied smile. 'Cos let's be honest, Alice Jane Wu, Grade Three with Merit – it really *is*, isn't it?'

THE GIFT

Written by Scott Handcock

Illustrated by Ashling Lindsay

Every year on Christmas Eve, Maisie Thompson would gaze out of her bedroom window at the vast, starry sky above her, watching out for Santa and his sleigh – although she'd never yet caught sight of either.

This year, snow was falling. It never snowed on Christmas Eve.

Maybe it's a sign, Maisie thought. *Perhaps this will be the year I finally get to meet him.*

All she had to do was stay awake.

She fixated on the world beyond the glass, watching as the snow started to settle. A thin layer formed at first, and grew steadily thicker, sparkling like a mass of fallen crystal as night fell.

Maisie smiled as the snowflakes drifted past. They'd travelled so far – and there were so many of them! Like visitors to Earth from another world. Millions, maybe even billions, of individuals, each as unique and fragile as the next.

She could have easily sat and watched them for hours. Perhaps she did. Either way, she was so rapt that she failed to notice the tall blue box that had appeared from nowhere a short way down the street. The thing that eventually distracted Maisie was a throng of carol-singers marching towards her house. They trudged along the pavement, wrapped in coats and scarves and smiles, spreading their festive cheer from door to door. She could hear their boisterous singing and now realised she had been humming along with each song.

'Deck the Halls', 'O Come, All Ye Faithful', 'God Rest You Merry, Gentlemen' . . . They were starting 'Silent Night' by the time they reached the Thompsons' front door.

Maisie rushed downstairs just as her mother unlocked the door. A wave of song washed over them.

'*All is calm, all is bright . . .*'

Maisie smiled and shivered slightly, moving closer to her mother as a chill wind crept inside.

'*Holy infant, so tender and mild . . .*'

Maisie's mother ruffled her hair as she joined in with the

final line, singing softly under her breath.

'*Sleep in heavenly peace.*'

Maisie and her mother clapped and cheered, and Maisie's mother reached into her purse. Then, with just as much cheer as when they had arrived, the carol-singers promptly dispersed into the night, this time to the tune of 'Hark! The Herald Angels Sing'.

But there was one voice which continued to sing in front of the Thompsons' house. Not quite a Christmas carol, but rather an impromptu and slightly inaccurate rendition of 'For He's A Jolly Good Fellow'.

The voice belonged to a young man dressed in a purple frock coat with a bow-tie, shirt and braces, sturdy boots and trousers so skinny they looked like his legs must have been sewn into them that morning. He had a childlike, friendly face, a prominent chin and a festive bobble hat on his head, topping off his strange ensemble.

'*For he's a jolly good fellow!*' he sang with gusto, dropping to his knees. Then he threw his arms wide and belted out the final lyric like a singer in a rock band. '*Aaaaand so say all of us!*' he howled, then bowed his head.

Maisie clapped appreciatively as the young man picked himself up from the ground, brushing ice from the front of his knees.

'Thank you, thank you,' he said. 'And no, I don't do encores. Sorry to disappoint!' He tugged at the bobble hat on his head. 'I'm the Doctor, incidentally. Hello! Happy Christmas! I wonder if you can help me?'

Maisie's mother reached into her purse.

'I'm afraid I don't have a lot of change,' she told him, rummaging around.

'Oh, I'm sorry to hear that,' said the Doctor, delving deep into the pockets of his coat. 'Will this do?' He poured a pile of coins into her hand. 'Should come to just under, oooh, thirty pounds, I think. More or less. Well, less. It's twenty-eight pounds and thirty-nine pence. Well, twenty-eight pounds, thirty-nine pence and a random euro. Still, everyone's been really rather generous. Except for the woman who lives at number seventeen, but then, between you and me, I think her hearing aid was probably on the blink. She kept putting her fingers in her ears. Anyway, like I said, I need your help.'

He reached back inside his coat, and plucked out a long, thin metal tube.

Maisie's mother looked alarmed. 'What's that?'

'Sonic screwdriver,' answered the Doctor, opening it with a flick of his wrist. With a sudden screech of noise, its tip glowed green and it started to pulse in a steady rhythm.

The Doctor held it to his ear and listened, monitoring the signal and tweaking the settings.

'Are you going to sing another song?' asked Maisie hopefully.

'Maybe later,' the Doctor said, whirling the sonic round from left to right. When he aimed it at the Thompsons' home, it began to bleep with fierce intensity.

'Aha!' the Doctor cried, closing the sonic shut with a gentle slam on the palm of his hand. 'Just as I thought. It's retreated somewhere warm. Now it's somewhere inside your home . . .'

Maisie's mother began to slowly shut the door.

'I should probably close this now,' she told him. 'It's cold enough as it is –'

The Doctor sneaked inside before she could finish.

'Couldn't agree more!' he said, glancing about the hallway. 'Where's it got to, I wonder?'

Maisie's mother looked appalled. 'You're in our home!'

'I know.' The Doctor beamed, oblivious to her outrage. 'Can't say I care for the wallpaper. Have you got any biscuits? No, never mind that now. Job to do. Sorry. Keep getting distracted.'

Maisie's mother ushered her daughter upstairs, then confronted the Doctor again.

'I'm warning you,' she told him calmly. 'If you don't leave right now, I'm calling the police!'

'They won't be able to help you,' he replied, still studying the sonic. 'They wouldn't have a clue how to deal with it.'

Maisie's mother had already picked up the phone. 'Deal with *what*?' she asked.

Suddenly from upstairs came the sound of Maisie's scream.

'With that,' he answered, bounding quickly up the stairs. 'Come on!'

When they entered Maisie's room, she was curled up in a corner of her bed, peering out from behind a duvet. Her face was frozen in an expression of panic. She couldn't speak, so instead pointed across the room.

There, a strange, otherworldly creature hopped about merrily. It could only have been three feet tall. Its face was shrewd and vicious, and it was dressed in ragged clothes, its skin a dull grey. Small, black eyes gleamed above its nose, and its laugh exposed a row of sharp, bright teeth.

Maisie's mum shrieked at the sight of it, but the noise didn't seem to bother the creature. It was too preoccupied wolfing down the cookies and carrots that Maisie had left out for Santa and his reindeer. Crumbs fell from its mouth as it chomped – its table manners certainly left a lot to be desired.

Maisie's mother's voice caught in the back of her throat. 'What is that thing?' she gasped.

'A Lengo,' answered the Doctor. The creature cocked its head upon hearing the name. 'Mischievous little creatures. Utterly harmless, of course. If anything, they just make a lot of noise!'

As if to prove him right, the Lengo guffawed in short, sharp bursts, before jumping on to Maisie's desk and scattering the contents of her pencil case on the floor. Then it laughed even harder.

'Oh, and mess,' the Doctor added apologetically. 'Should have mentioned that. Noise and mess – the two things they like to make. But don't worry! I'm here to help, and hopefully get him back where he belongs.'

'Is it a monster?' Maisie asked.

The Doctor laughed. 'Nah, not this little critter. Look at him!'

The Doctor coaxed the Lengo closer. 'Come on, boy!' he said softly. 'Let's leave the nice people be now. Come on, come to me . . .'

Slowly, the Doctor shuffled towards the Lengo.

'Where did it come from?' Maisie's mother hissed.

'From a very long way away. A planet called Lengos

Four. Which is odd, thinking about it, because there are only two other planets in the system.'

Still gently approaching the Lengo, the Doctor pulled out his sonic screwdriver. 'Take a look at this for me, would you?' He waved the sonic gently back and forth in front of the Lengo, and the creature's eyes followed it. The Doctor seemed to whisper a lullaby, and the Lengo's eyelids began to droop. A few moments later, they heard the creature snoring. Loudly.

'There we go,' said the Doctor, clapping his hands. 'Should snooze for a few more minutes, which gives me plenty of time to do *this*!'

The sonic emitted a high-pitched whine as he aimed it at Maisie's bed. She felt it before she saw it: a warm wave of energy pulsing towards her, then a tiny point of light churning round and round to form a portal.

Through it, they could see another world, blurred and indistinct. On the other side of the portal, voices chittered in short, staccato shots, sounding just like the Lengo in Maisie's bedroom.

'It's a wormhole,' the Doctor explained. 'This little fellow must have sneaked through it by mistake and ended up here.'

Maisie's mother looked aghast. 'A wormhole in our house? You can't be serious!'

'Never, if I can help it.' The Doctor grinned, hoisting the

Lengo into his arms and through the portal, then setting it down safely on the other side.

He pulled out his sonic again, aiming it once more at the wormhole. After a short, shrill burst of noise, the portal began to spin in the other direction. It turned and whirled, growing smaller and smaller and smaller, until eventually it collapsed and vanished entirely.

Maisie's mother was lost for words. Too many questions were flooding through her head, and she couldn't quite decide which was most important.

Instead, her daughter got there first. 'Was that an alien then?' she asked, far less scared than she had been earlier.

The Doctor stopped in his tracks.

'Yes, it was.' He smiled. 'And so am I. But don't worry, I'm one of the good ones!'

He slipped the sonic back inside his pocket and turned to Maisie's mother. 'I don't suppose you'd mind showing me the door?'

Oddly, she was more than happy to oblige.

'Bye, then!' cried the Doctor, as Maisie's mother ushered him outside. 'And happy Christmas to you both!'

He waved with both his hands, sighing contentedly as the door shut softly behind him. Everything had gone according to plan. Which the Doctor thought was great, considering he hadn't actually had a plan to start with.

He walked through the blizzard with his arms outstretched, enjoying the satisfying crunch of the snow beneath his feet. At the end of the street, he could see the TARDIS, its panels blazing brightly through a delicate sheen of frost.

The Doctor could still see Maisie, too – she was sitting on the inner windowsill of her bedroom, just as she had been earlier. He smiled and waved but, to his surprise, Maisie didn't smile back. In fact, she was frowning.

'Is there something wrong?' the Doctor called.

Maisie checked over her shoulder, then opened the window.

'It's the Lengo,' she said in a sniffling voice, wiping her eyes with the end of her sleeve. 'Mum says it took some of our presents. The ones she kept on top of the wardrobe. She's on the phone to Nana but it's too late to get any new ones . . .'

The Doctor considered this for a moment, before a smile spread across his face.

'Gimme a sec!' he yelled, disappearing from Maisie's vision.

Seconds later he was climbing up one of the drainpipes.

'Won't be a tick,' he huffed, clambering unsteadily

upwards. 'What's your name, by the way?'

'Maisie,' she replied. 'My name is Maisie Elizabeth Thompson.'

The Doctor smiled. 'That's a good name, Maisie Elizabeth Thompson. Three good names, in fact. Aren't you lucky?'

With one hand free, he rummaged in his pocket, then passed Maisie the sonic screwdriver. 'Here, take this!'

He winced, then threw himself unceremoniously across to the window ledge.

There wasn't any way to make an entrance like this with dignity, so the Doctor didn't even try. He heaved himself through the window and fell in a heap of sprawling limbs on Maisie's floor. He then promptly leaped to his feet and dusted himself down.

'Front doors are boring, don't you think? Screwdriver, please,' he said, holding out a hand.

Obediently, Maisie passed it to him.

'I should still have the settings programmed in,' he said, aiming the sonic at the very same spot from earlier. 'All we need to do now is reopen the wormhole, go to the Lengo's planet, find where he's stashed your presents, get them off him, maybe fit in the odd bit of sightseeing, then we can come back here, close the wormhole and pop the presents under the tree before milk and biscuits! How does that sound?'

'You said "we" – does that mean I'm coming with you?' Maisie asked, her eyes wide.

The Doctor nodded. 'I'll look after you, I promise,' he said. 'And, as I said earlier, the Lengoes are harmless.'

'But I'm in my pyjamas!'

'Oh, the Lengoes won't mind that. They're not remotely fashion-conscious!'

He smiled as he flicked the sonic's handle, and the wormhole began to open once again. The air around Maisie and the Doctor twisted, distending and distorting above the bed. Gradually, the image through the portal started to appear, revealing the world beyond.

The Doctor offered Maisie a reassuring hand. 'Shall we go then?' he asked.

Maisie hesitated. 'What about Mum?'

'Oh, of course!' he said, as if the thought hadn't occurred to him. 'Do you think she'd want to come too?'

'No! I mean, what if she comes in and realises I'm not here?'

'We'll be quick,' the Doctor promised. 'Cross my hearts. I've got a time machine parked just down the road!'

First aliens and wormholes, now time machines . . .

Maisie wondered if she should really trust the Doctor. He was certainly odd, but he said that he'd look after her, and he'd already saved them from the Lengo once . . . Besides, how many people could say they'd actually been to an alien planet? This was without a doubt a once-in-a-lifetime opportunity.

Making up her mind, Maisie nodded and took the Doctor's hand. Together they stepped through the burning hoop of light.

Passing through the wormhole was a bit like walking through a very thin film of jelly. It was momentarily oppressive – Maisie could feel the tensions between realities pressing against her – then it gave way to another world. A totally different point in space and time.

It was unlike anything Maisie had ever seen, or even imagined.

They'd arrived in a sort of alleyway. Maisie could see several Lengoes scampering through the streets of the town that lay ahead of them, chittering and chattering as they went about their business. Normality on a far-from-normal world.

She took a deep breath to steady herself and cold air filled her nostrils. It was freezing here.

'Lengos Four.' The Doctor grinned. 'We made it!'

He studied the sonic screwdriver, adjusting its settings.

'Travelling through wormholes always leaves a bit of temporal–spatial residue,' he said. 'Meaning we should be able to track down your little friend quite quickly.'

The screwdriver started to buzz and hum excitedly.

'Aha! It's not gone far at all . . . This way, I think.'

With that, the Doctor strode off down the alleyway, leaving Maisie trailing in his wake.

When they emerged on to the street that lay beyond the alleyway, Maisie was overwhelmed by the alien world around her. Two dazzlingly bright moons hung above in a blood-red sky, and huge, silvery shapes fluttered down from the clouds. One bright shard softly grazed Maisie's cheek, then melted clean away.

The Doctor cheered, catching a single, massive flake in the palm of his hand. He held it out to Maisie for approval.

'Snow!' she cried.

'It *is* snow.' He laughed, blowing the giant snowflake off his hand. Another one tickled the tip of his nose. 'Blimey, nothing gets past you, does it?'

As they walked on, the Doctor threw out his arms, gesturing to the Lengo town around them. 'Just look at it here! Isn't it *brilliant?*'

Maisie couldn't deny it. Yes, this world was cold and strange, but it was also extremely beautiful. And not like visiting an art gallery on a school trip, where she said everything looked great because she felt like she had to. No, this was an instant, honest acknowledgement. Something about this place took her breath away.

She watched as a layer of snow lightly began to dust the town's streets, which were made of a stony material that reminded Maisie of a coral reef. The buildings looked organic, as though they'd been carefully cultivated over several millennia. Every one was different in shape and size, but each had been nurtured from the same coral and crimson stone.

Pale stones lined the streets and pillars stretched skyward from the pavements – some high into the heavens, others twisted into elegant arcs between the buildings, but all seemed to shine with an enchanted light.

'Natural phosphorescence,' explained the Doctor, catching Maisie's eye. Not that this explained much; he might as well have said 'It's magic!' for all Maisie understood.

They wandered along the streets and through crowds of Lengoes. All the while, the Doctor monitored the bleeps and whirrs from his sonic screwdriver.

'Not far now,' he told Maisie – though, truthfully, she was

so busy drinking in every detail of the alien world around her that she'd forgotten all about the presents.

Everywhere they walked, they passed Lengoes of all kinds. Some were young; some were old. Some wore rags, while others were dressed in fancy frocks. Not one of them looked the same as another.

There was one Lengo, no more than a foot in height, toddling absent-mindedly through the throng. It had to be a baby, Maisie thought, but she couldn't see any grown-up Lengoes with it.

She watched for a while, then tugged on the Doctor's sleeve.

'Can we help it find its parents?' she asked.

'I'm afraid not,' the Doctor told her. 'Lengoes aren't like humans. They don't really have families or friends. Mostly they just fend for themselves. That's why they're all so polite to each other! They've spent millennia after millennia having to appear tolerable to one another, just to survive. Sometimes they get bored of all that politeness and become a bit mischievous.'

Maisie looked around at the flurry of Lengoes. There were so many of them. Each of them alone. 'That's so sad,' she said quietly.

'No, it isn't,' the Doctor reassured her. 'They've never

known anything different. Trust me, they're perfectly happy
the way they are!'

Maisie couldn't argue. The Doctor knew this world
better than she did. But, somehow, she felt in her heart that
she was right: the Lengoes were missing out, even if they
didn't realise it.

'Here we are,' said the Doctor, interrupting her train of
thought.

They'd reached a short, squat door carved into the front
of one of the buildings. The Doctor knocked on it and, after
a moment or two of clattering from within, a figure answered.

It was the Lengo from Maisie's bedroom. It seemed to
recognise them instantly, burbling nervously in what Maisie
guessed to be a combination of thrill and panic.

'I'll take care of this,' the Doctor told her, straightening
his bow-tie as if he meant business. He squatted on his heels,
meeting the Lengo eye-to-eye, and issued a peculiar babble
of throaty noises. 'I speak Lengo, by the way,' he told Maisie
helpfully.

Maisie stared at him incredulously as the Lengo
responded with a sequence of excited chatter. He seemed
quite agitated.

The Doctor responded.

The Lengo then frowned and replied slowly.

Has the Doctor offended him? Maisie wondered as she watched it scamper back inside its dwelling.

'He didn't realise,' the Doctor told her. 'As I said, they don't do the family thing, so it never occurred to him that those presents might have been *important*. Sentimental value isn't a big concept on Lengos Four.'

The Lengo returned to the door, dwarfed beneath the large stack of gifts he was holding. He chittered at the Doctor once again.

'He says he's sorry,' said the Doctor, translating. 'And . . . and he wishes to extend to you greetings of festive cheer!'

The Doctor helped Maisie to retrieve the gifts from the Lengo's arms, and patted him on the head. Then he turned to Maisie. 'Shall we go?'

Maisie shook her head. 'I'm not quite ready yet.'

The Doctor watched as she sifted through the pile of presents, settling on one of the largest, addressed to her. She offered it back to the Lengo.

'It's a present,' she said. 'For you. I want you to have it.'

The Lengo looked confused and turned to the Doctor, who translated with a series of guttural barks from the back of his throat. The Lengo, appearing to understand, accepted the gift from Maisie, then seemed to sniff and spluttered some grateful words.

This time, Maisie didn't need the Doctor to translate.

'You're welcome,' she told the Lengo softly, pulling it in for a hug. 'Merry Christmas.'

The Doctor and Maisie left the Lengo alone that night. Alone, but perhaps no longer lonely.

They travelled back to Maisie's bedroom through the wormhole, clutching the Thompsons' presents between them. The Doctor then scurried back down the drainpipe instead of using the door – front doors were still boring, he maintained – and Maisie watched as he disappeared into a tall, blue wooden box at the end of her street.

The box soon vanished, fading in and out until it disappeared entirely from the blizzard, and Maisie Elizabeth Thompson wondered if she would ever see the Doctor again.

Thirty-four years later, Maisie Elizabeth Hussain was enjoying a quiet Christmas at home. She was married now, with two children – a boy and a girl – and Christmas was a special time, just as it had been when she was small.

Much to her surprise, a carol-singer arrived on her doorstep on Christmas Eve, dressed in a familiar combination of bow-tie, festive bobble hat and frock coat. Maisie recognised him instantly. She also recognised the tall, blue box that was standing behind him.

The Doctor wasted no time in telling Maisie excitedly that her simple gesture of generosity all those years before had gone on to change Lengo society. With one small act of giving, she had turned an entire world upside-down.

The Lengo they met had wanted to share Maisie's generosity. He had sought to include others in his life and began to pass on gifts, realising the gift of giving as well as receiving. Maisie's goodwill had infected the planet like a virus.

Now, almost three decades later, the Lengoes had a Christmas-like festival of their own. They were united instead of alone, celebrating their lives in each other's company.

'I'd like to take you back to Lengos Four,' said the Doctor. 'I want to show you what you achieved, without ever even knowing.'

Maisie smiled. *This is a once-in-a-lifetime opportunity*, she reminded herself. Another once-in-a-lifetime opportunity, if such a thing were possible.

'I just need to fetch a few things,' she told the Doctor, rushing upstairs. Moments later, she returned with her husband and two children in tow. Each of them was confused, and none of them had their shoes on, but Maisie knew from experience that it wouldn't matter. There was no way they could miss out on this.

And so, together, the Hussains ventured into a battered old time machine and travelled to another world. A world across the cosmos. They celebrated Christmas alongside an alien civilisation that now, thanks to Maisie, understood the spirit of Christmas.

Hers was truly a gift that kept on giving.

THE PERSISTENCE
OF MEMORY

Written by Colin Brake

Illustrated by Tom Duxbury

The boy looked around in astonishment at the impossible room, which was somehow *inside* the old-fashioned police telephone box he had just entered. He was determined to imprint every detail on his memory. The room was circular, with a central column filled with bars of golden light. A six-sided control panel covered with dials, read-outs and levers encircled the lit column, and a couple of the panels were topped with screens. Around the walls of the room was a sort of observation platform, which housed bookshelves, trinkets and a chalk blackboard on which the single word 'Spangles' was written.

'Go on, then. Say it. Everyone does.'

The speaker was a slim man with a shock of grey hair,

a well-lined face and the fiercest eyebrows the boy had ever seen outside of a horror comic. CJ – he preferred to use his initials rather than his given name – was perhaps not your usual fourteen-year-old boy from South London. While most of the other boys at school collected and swapped football cards or superhero comics, CJ had a more curious hobby.

He collected *mysteries*.

He had already filled three large scrapbooks with magazine and newspaper cuttings about mysterious events and places, and it was the pursuit of a new one that had led him here to this . . . whatever it was.

The man with the eyebrows was gesticulating with his hand. 'Blah, blah, bigger on the inside, blah, blah . . . Come on, lad, make an effort! It's called the TARDIS.'

Somehow, CJ managed to find his voice. 'It's a spaceship, isn't it? No, *more* than that – a *time* ship!'

The stranger stopped his hand-waving and looked impressed.

CJ had first seen the man about ten minutes earlier in Mr Singh's newsagent's. Just for a change, Slade's 'Merry Christmas, Everybody' had been on the radio. CJ was properly sick of the six-year-old tune; he hoped it would finally be forgotten about by next year.

Trying to ignore the song's noisy chorus, CJ had been

eyeing up a newspaper's front page. It proclaimed to have an exclusive feature on the Loch Ness Monster – with brand-new pictures of the monster itself! CJ knew he had to add it to his scrapbook, but he didn't have any money.

The stranger had been in the shop, buying a packet of sweets – some fizzy orange Spangles. He was obviously a regular, as Mr Singh had called him 'Doctor'.

CJ picked up the paper he wanted and was trying to tuck it inside his jacket, when he heard the Doctor say something peculiar. He was telling Mr Singh that he made a point of coming here to buy Spangles, but when Mr Singh pointed out that other shops sold the sweets the Doctor had corrected him; by 'here', he meant the year, not the shop, he had said. 'You try getting these in the twenty-first century,' he had told the shopkeeper.

CJ had been so shocked that he had dropped the paper he was attempting to steal. To his surprise, the stranger had walked over and picked it up for him.

'Here,' he said, handing CJ the paper and a ten-pence coin, with a knowing smile.

CJ had been surprised at the man's generous gesture, but not as surprised as he was when he looked down at the coin in his hand. The coin was dated 1987 – eight years in the future!

Forgetting the newspaper, CJ had pulled the shop

door open and run outside. There had been no sign of the mysterious Doctor in either direction, so CJ had checked the alleyway behind the shops. As he rounded the corner, he was surprised to see the old-fashioned police box blocking the road. The Doctor was stepping into it.

CJ was not particularly sporty at the best of times, but he had set off towards it like an Olympic sprinter. The light on the top of the police box had begun to flash, and an unearthly mechanical noise had filled the air. To CJ's astonishment, the box appeared to be fading from view. For a split second, he thought he might pass straight through it, like a ghost – then the doors had solidified and he had crashed through them, rolling into the impossible space beyond.

As he staggered to his feet, CJ had found himself facing the Doctor in the enormous circular room.

'The coin you gave me in Mr Singh's – it was from the future,' he said, with growing confidence. 'And so are you!'

He ventured a little further into the room. The steady hum of what sounded like a great engine came from somewhere deep below.

'What kind of a pudding-brain throws himself at a dematerialising TARDIS?' the Doctor asked, shaking his head.

CJ shrugged and smiled cautiously. 'A curious one?' He offered his hand for the Doctor to shake. 'My name is CJ.'

The Doctor sighed, ignored CJ's hand and began studying one of the instrument panels. 'I suppose I'll have to take you right back to nineteen seventy-nine,' he muttered. 'I could just use the fast-return switch, I suppose.' He reached for a large red lever.

'Wait!' shouted CJ.

The Doctor stopped and looked at him.

'It's Christmas – a time for generosity! Can't you take me on one quick trip? I bet you could get me back to this exact time and place afterwards, couldn't you?'

The Doctor couldn't help but smile. Adult humans often frustrated him with their closed-mindedness, but he had always found younger humans to be much more interest*ing* and interest*ed*.

'OK, since it's Christmas. One trip. Anywhere in time and space,' the Doctor said. 'That's the deal. I have a friend who usually travels with me, but she's off enjoying something called an "end-of-term Christmas party", so I'm at a loose end. Where's it to be?'

CJ thought for a moment of all the clippings in his scrapbooks. He'd been collecting them for years: tales of Big Foot or Sasquatch, of Yeti in the Himalayas and panthers roaming Dartmoor. And it wasn't just strange beasts he was interested in – he had clippings on the Bermuda Triangle, space travellers on Inca temples, UFO sightings over Roswell . . .

'How about the *Mary Celeste*?' CJ finally suggested, remembering the tale of the mysteriously abandoned ship found adrift in 1872.

'Boring,' said the Doctor. 'That was the Daleks.'

'Erm . . . Stonehenge, when it was being built?'

'Been there, done that,' said the Doctor. 'And that's no mystery. Just aliens.'

'OK then, how about the Loch Ness Monster?' CJ offered, crossing his fingers for luck.

'Well, there was the Zygons' pet Skarasen which turned up in the Thames that time,' muttered the Doctor. 'Has that happened yet? I'm always a bit vague on the dates.'

'I don't know anything about Zygons,' replied CJ. 'But I do know there were lots of new Nessie sightings reported this summer.'

'Loch Ness in the summer of nineteen seventy-nine it is then,' declared the Doctor, turning and setting the controls. 'Let's go and find ourselves a wee, tim'rous beastie, shall we?'

When the doors to the TARDIS opened again, Mr Singh's newsagent's was nowhere to be seen. The police box had materialised beside a vast expanse of calm blue water, which

CJ guessed was the famous Loch Ness. Tree-covered hills rose up from the opposite side of the lake and, further away, CJ could see the remains of a castle towering above the water.

'Scotland in August.' The Doctor sighed as they stepped outside, closing the door of the TARDIS behind him. 'Nowhere finer.'

It had been midday when CJ had entered the TARDIS, but here it was beginning to grow dark. The Doctor started off towards the water's edge and CJ hurried after him. A short distance away, CJ could see a small encampment – a couple of tents pitched around a campfire. A young man of around twenty emerged from one of the tents.

'Hi,' said the camper, with a friendly expression. 'Are you looking for the old girl?'

'Old girl?' said CJ.

'Nessie!'

The youth, who gave his name as Robbie, explained that he and his friends were Nessie hunters. Every year they came to Loch Ness and set up a camp here, hoping to spot the mysterious monster. Robbie's two friends had gone into the nearest town for supplies, leaving him alone on watch.

'Have you ever seen the monster?' asked CJ, sitting down by the fire.

'Not myself,' confessed Robbie, 'but my friend Al saw

something just the other night. He managed to get a photo.'
The young Nessie hunter reached into his pocket and
produced a Polaroid photograph.

The Doctor glanced at it, narrowing his fierce eyebrows,
then passed it on to CJ. The photograph had been taken at
night and, despite the camera's built-in flash, the resulting
image was far from clear.

'Where exactly was this taken?' asked the Doctor.

'Not far from the camp,' Robbie answered, pointing to
where the edge of the loch curved away from them. 'I'll show
you,' he added brightly, getting to his feet.

Robbie led the Doctor and CJ to a ridge of land that
jutted into the loch. The three of them looked out over the
smooth water. A ripple appeared on the surface.

'Is it me, or is something moving out there?' CJ asked,
his voice trembling.

'I see it too!' said Robbie excitedly. 'Would you look at
that now!'

The water was definitely moving, a short distance from
where they stood. Waves appeared, small at first, then larger
and larger. Then something huge exploded out of the water,
and CJ almost jumped into the air in fright. Whatever the
thing was, it immediately dived beneath the surface again
before anyone could get a good look at it.

Robbie looked like he might explode from excitement. 'Did you see that?' he cried, turning to the Doctor and CJ with his eyes wide.

Before Robbie could go on, it happened again. This time, they got a better look at the enormous creature – CJ spotted a long neck and scaly skin as the creature reared up, sending cascades of water in all directions, before it returned once more to the deep.

Robbie looked at them triumphantly. 'See, she *is* real! She looked like some kind of dinosaur!'

'A Plesiosaurus,' CJ corrected him, his heart racing. 'A genus of extinct, large marine reptiles that lived during the early part of the Jurassic period.' He had discovered the secret of Nessie – this day would need a whole scrapbook of its own!

Robbie ran closer to the edge of the water. 'Quick, get the camera!' he called back. CJ saw an expensive-looking Polaroid on a box beside Robbie's folding chair.

'Robbie, get back!' warned the Doctor.

But he was too late.

The creature burst up from the depths for a third time, unleashing a wave that knocked the poor Nessie hunter off his feet. Robbie slipped and fell into the water, splashing wildly.

Before either the Doctor or CJ could do or say anything,

something peculiar happened – an explosion of light, as if a flare had been set off, followed by a strange electronic noise.

CJ blinked, seeing flashes before his eyes, but the effect quickly faded. With surprise, he noticed that there was no longer any sign of the sea monster in the loch. It had completely disappeared. All that was left was poor Robbie, swimming with difficulty in the rough waters.

The Doctor had already moved to grab an emergency lifebuoy from a nearby post. He threw it to Robbie and, with CJ's help, hauled the lad back to solid ground. The Doctor then quickly checked that Robbie hadn't sustained any injuries, and determined that he was fine, if rather wet and cold.

'Get yourself dry, and keep away from the loch,' the Doctor said, striding off. 'Come on,' he urged CJ.

'Where are we going?'

'Back to the TARDIS.'

CJ wondered if time travel always involved this much running. Puffing a little, he jogged as quickly as he could up the hill after the Doctor.

Inside the TARDIS, the Doctor was already at the controls, running some checks.

'As I suspected,' the Doctor told CJ, who was leaning on the console trying to catch his breath. 'There's a residual trace of artron energy.'

'Which means what?'

'When something travels through the space–time vortex, it leaves a trail of artron particles,' explained the Doctor. He pulled down a lever and flicked a couple of switches. 'And this particular trail leads . . . here!'

The Doctor activated a view screen, which showed them grey, metallic walls.

'Where are we?'

'According to the TARDIS, we're inside a very large spaceship, which is sitting on the bottom of the loch,' the Doctor told CJ.

'There's an alien spaceship at the bottom of Loch Ness?' CJ said with excitement, despite his fear. 'What kind of alien spaceship? Friendly aliens? Not-friendly aliens?'

'Not sure,' said the Doctor, frowning. 'But there's one thing I do know. This is the location of the device that took that poor creature from the loch – some kind of primitive Time Scoop.' He started to walk towards the doors. 'And we need to find whoever is responsible.'

The Doctor and CJ stepped out of the TARDIS into a metal-walled corridor. There was a cold efficiency to the design – flat grey panels and silvery steel mouldings, with muted blue lighting. The corridor was gently curved, reminding CJ of his favourite TV programme.

'Bit *Star Trek*, isn't it?' suggested CJ, peering around the corridor as they walked along it.

'If you say so,' replied the Doctor. 'It's more reminiscent of a Dalek ship, if you ask me.'

Abruptly the Doctor stopped and turned to CJ, with a finger to his lips. Ahead of them, the corridor opened up into a cavernous area four or five times the size of the TARDIS control room. Mammoth equipment filled the space – power lines and control panels attached to something that looked like an oversized desk lamp with a long, gun-like barrel where the bulb should be.

'That's the Time Scoop,' whispered the Doctor. 'Just as I thought . . .'

The corridor led out to a circular walkway, which ran all the way round the wall of the chamber, a ramp on each side descending to ground level. Along the walkway were alcoves containing display cases full of curios and collectibles.

Two figures appeared on either side of the walkway: large security robots with what looked like weapons built into their arms. Their heads were spherical, capable of swivelling a full 360 degrees, and they moved slowly and purposefully in opposite directions across the chamber.

The Doctor beckoned CJ into one of the alcoves and they ducked down to hide behind a display case.

'Are they in charge?' whispered CJ.

The Doctor shook his head. 'I doubt it. They match the design of the ship – I'd say they're just automated crew. I'm more interested in whoever wrote their programs.'

One of the patrolling robots passed their hiding place and returned to its starting position. Then, both robots made a whirring noise and stopped moving, as if powering down.

'Whatever happens, keep out of sight,' said the Doctor firmly, then he moved quietly out of the alcove and ran down one of the ramps.

CJ wondered where the Doctor was going – the seconds that ticked by in his absence felt like an eternity. When seconds then became minutes, CJ began to wonder if the Doctor was ever coming back. He couldn't see anything from his hiding place – perhaps if he just crept carefully to the walkway he'd be able to see what was going on.

Remembering the Doctor's warning, CJ cautiously crawled out from behind the display case and on to the walkway.

The vast hall was empty, with no sign of life. On the floor below, CJ could see some screens, which were connected to the machine the Doctor had called a Time Scoop – dozens of them, all showing different scenes.

CJ gulped with excitement as he realised what the
screens were showing: not different TV stations, but different
places in history. Even from this distance he could make out
dinosaurs on one and something that looked like a half-built
pyramid on another. Curiosity quickly got the better of him,
and he edged forward to get a closer look.

Keeping an eye out for any movement, CJ stepped down
the nearest ramp towards the screens. As he got closer, he saw
more details – a Roman army marching, a pirate ship, some
kind of giant wheel on the banks of the Thames . . . It wasn't
just the past on the screens, he realised. It was the future too!

One of the screens showed some kind of invasion. At
first, CJ thought the invaders were zombies, but then he
realised they were shop dummies – moving mannequins with
concealed weapons on their wrists.

'Now, what do we have here?' said a strange voice in
sing-song tones. 'Did I pick up a hitchhiker when I scooped
up my Nessie?'

CJ spun round and saw that a peculiar man had
appeared behind him. He was powerfully built and wore a
richly decorated scarlet robe, which was tied with a paisley-
patterned scarf as a belt. On his feet were practical-looking
boots, similar to the chunky-soled shoes that the Doctor was

wearing. Unlike the robots, which matched the ship in design and feel, the stranger seemed out of place here.

'I'm lost,' said CJ lamely.

'I rather think you are,' agreed the stranger. 'Perhaps I should send you back to the Jurassic era with our scaly friend?'

'I don't think that's a very good idea,' said an angry voice. CJ looked past the stranger and was delighted to see the Doctor descending from the opposite ramp.

'You can't go around sending innocent people through time,' said the Doctor, clearly furious, as he reached the ground floor. 'Who are you? Where did you get this time technology?'

The man just looked at the Doctor and laughed. He had wide blue eyes that seemed to sparkle with amusement, and CJ could see deep laughter lines on his face. Whoever he was, he was clearly someone who found plenty to laugh at in life.

'Me?' he asked, pointing at his own chest. 'I'm just a traveller. And a collector. Much like yourself.'

'A collector? Me?' The Doctor was clearly surprised by the turn of the conversation. He shook his head and looked over at CJ. 'Are you all right, CJ?'

CJ tried hard to sound like he wasn't afraid. 'Never better, Doctor.'

'Good,' said the Doctor. 'Listen to me and I promise I'll

get you out of here.'

'Oh, don't make promises you can't keep, Doctor,' warned the stranger.

The Doctor turned and approached the man, anger burning in his eyes.

'Now, listen here. You need to shut down this Time Scoop and stop meddling with things you don't understand. Time travel is not a game. You don't play with time. You don't scoop up marine creatures from millions of years ago and drop them into Loch Ness for a laugh.'

The illegal Time-Scoop operator laughed again. 'Who's going to stop me? The Time Lords? Aren't they too busy hiding from their own shadows these days?'

The Doctor suddenly seemed unsettled. 'What do you know about the Time Lords?' he demanded.

'Oh, Doctor – you change your face, but you don't change your ways. You're just as naïve and boring as you've ever been. Don't you ever learn? Meddling is always fun. What's the point in anything if there's no mischief?'

CJ was shocked to see the colour draining from the Doctor's face.

'It can't be you . . .' he stammered.

'You're not the only one wearing a new face, Doctor,' said the man, spinning round as if showing off a new outfit. 'It's me, Mortimus! What did you call me once? The Meddling Monk? Well, I've ditched the monk look. You could say I've got a new habit!' He laughed. 'Do you get it? Habit?' He giggled again, then realised he was laughing alone. 'Oh, never mind.'

Suddenly the security robots appeared again, this time at the top of each ramp.

'Robots, escort our guests to the cells,' ordered the Monk.

The robots moved forward and CJ flinched, expecting a cold metallic hand to grab him at any moment.

But nothing happened.

'Hey! What do you think you're doing?'

CJ opened his eyes and saw that the two robots were holding the Monk captive, instead of the Doctor.

'Sorry, old friend,' the Doctor said, a hint of amusement in his voice. 'I'm afraid you've got a mutiny on your hands. These boys work for me now!'

He waved something that looked like a rather over-designed multi-tool in the Monk's face. 'You never were very good at positronic brains, were you, M? Took me about ten seconds with my sonic screwdriver to hack into this ship's computer and replace you as commander.'

'You really are a killjoy, aren't you?' muttered the Monk,

raising his hands in defeat. 'Fine. You win, Doctor!'

But the Doctor wasn't finished. 'What mischief were you planning with this Time Scoop?' he demanded.

The Monk shrugged. 'I hadn't really decided,' he said airily. He explained that he had come across the abandoned ship far in the distant future, and had decided to take it for himself. 'I thought I might use it to depopulate this little planet that everyone values so much, and offer it up to the highest bidder. The Rutans, the Sontarans, maybe even the Daleks . . . There's no shortage of races that would pay a handsome price for planet Earth.'

The Doctor looked furious again, as CJ wondered aloud, 'What happens now, Doctor? Are you going to hand him over to the police?'

He seemed to consider this for a moment. 'Well, I could bring in the Shadow Proclamation, I suppose,' said the Doctor. CJ saw the Monk's grin fade rapidly at the suggestion, and the Doctor shook his head. 'No, I couldn't do that to him . . .'

The Doctor explained to CJ that the Monk was a fellow Time Lord – whatever that was – which meant that he too had a TARDIS. After a quick search of the room, they found the Monk's time machine disguised as a plain white wardrobe, hidden behind the Time-Scoop machinery.

To CJ's surprise, the Doctor decided that the best thing would be to let the Monk go.

'But we can't just let him get away with it!' CJ cried.

'He won't,' said the Doctor firmly. He returned to his TARDIS, then came back carrying a box – inside was a creature that looked like a giant worm.

The Monk looked scared. 'Not a memory worm, Doctor, please! You can't wipe my mind with that thing!'

'I think it would be best if you forget all about this ship,' said the Doctor firmly. 'One little bite from our friend here and you won't remember a thing!' He beckoned one of the service robots over – it picked up the worm from the box and carried it across to the Monk's neck.

With his short-term memory now a complete blank, the Monk was quickly bundled by the Doctor back into his wardrobe TARDIS. The Doctor set the controls, and a few moments later the Monk's TARDIS disappeared from view.

'What are you going to do about this ship? And the Time Scoop?' asked CJ. 'It's a bit dangerous to leave it here, isn't it?'

The Doctor agreed. 'Extremely. I'm going to program the robots to pilot it into the sun. That should see it safely destroyed.'

CJ nodded. 'I wonder what happened to the original

crew,' he said, hoping the Doctor would give an answer that wasn't too sad.

'The shielding on the Scoop is a bit suspect,' said the Doctor. 'I suspect there may have been a leakage of artron energy, causing a time disturbance that removed the crew from their own timelines.' He sighed, sounding tired. 'Time is a very dangerous thing to play around with, CJ. The Monk is lucky we came across him when we did – this thing might well have blown up in his face and caused a major timequake.'

The Doctor stopped and patted CJ on the shoulder. 'But never mind that, eh?' he said, with a small smile. 'Time to get you home, I think.'

Inside the TARDIS control room, the Doctor pottered around the central console, flicking switches and checking read-outs.

CJ watched him carefully. He couldn't stop thinking about the memory worm – the more he thought about it, the more he became convinced that the Doctor would use it on him too. This whole fantastic adventure could be stolen from his memory, and he'd never even know it . . .

While the Doctor was busy flying the TARDIS, CJ pulled out the notebook that he kept in his jacket pocket and began to sketch and make notes. When he heard a change in the engine sound – which he now knew meant the TARDIS was landing – he carefully slipped the notebook back into his pocket.

'Here we are then!' said the Doctor. 'London, December twenty-fourth, nineteen-seventy-nine, right? We've materialised about thirty seconds after we left.'

CJ's eyes drifted to the box containing the memory worm. 'Are you going to –' he began.

'Wipe your mind?' The Doctor laughed, but not entirely convincingly. 'No, no. Well, not with the memory worm. That's a bit of a blunt instrument. But I do need to blur some of the details.' He pressed a single bony finger to the middle of CJ's forehead. 'You saw glimpses of the future on the Monk's screens. And no one should know too much about their own future . . .'

CJ blinked, his thoughts a fuzzy mess. He wasn't even sure where he was for a moment. Looking around, he eventually realised he was standing in the alley behind Mr Singh's newsagent's. A fading echo of a strange wheezing sound was in the air – then all was silent. Shaking his head to clear the cobwebs, CJ began walking home.

He had a half memory of something incredible happening. Something to do with a blue box and time travel and someone called . . . the Doctor? Had it really happened, or had he read about it somewhere? The more he tried to remember the details, the fainter the memory became, until it felt more like a dream than a real event.

But that night, as he was getting into bed, CJ found something peculiar in his notebook. There were some scribbled notes about the Loch Ness Monster, which CJ couldn't remember writing, next to a sketch of an old-fashioned police box. It was labelled with the words 'time and space machine'. And two more words, written at the bottom of the page: 'The Doctor'.

What on earth could it mean? It was a mystery, but something totally new – not like the other things in CJ's scrapbooks. This deserved a whole new scrapbook of its own!

CJ woke up the next morning – *Christmas* morning! – and leaped downstairs, eager to open his presents. Tearing open the first one, he found a brand-new scrapbook, just as he'd hoped.

'For your next set of mysteries, Clive,' his nan said, smiling at the elated expression on CJ's face.

When all the presents had been opened, CJ retreated to his room to survey his new belongings. A cassette player, some felt-tips, a book about ancient myths . . . he'd done very well this year. But the best present hadn't come gift-wrapped at all. Opening his new scrapbook and using one of his new felt-tips, CJ labelled the cover:

THE MYSTERY OF THE DOCTOR AND THE BLUE BOX BY CLIVE J FINCH

It was the start of a fascination that would last for many years to come. Soon, Clive's scrapbook would become a collection of cuttings and photos, of sightings and mentions – the first of a dozen scrapbooks that eventually became a website. A site that would one day be discovered by a girl named Rose Tyler, after she too met a mysterious Doctor who travelled in a blue police box.

As the TARDIS spun through the time vortex, something stirred in the depths of the Doctor's mind. A fleeting memory – something Rose had told him about when he'd first met her, during that business with the Autons.

Rose had said that she'd found a website all about the Doctor and the TARDIS. A website run by a man of about forty named Clive . . . which would have made him about fourteen in 1979, just like the lad the Doctor had taken to Loch Ness.

It couldn't have been him, could it? The Doctor shook his head. Perhaps he was remembering it wrong. Perhaps that website had been run by a man called Dave or Kevin.

The Doctor sighed and thought of some wise words a friend of his had once written: *Time is the thief of memory.*

How true, he thought, as his magical ship slipped between the present and the past, between tomorrow and yesterday, between the not-yet-now and the not-quite-then. Time is infinite, but memory is not. All memories fade, in time.